DANNY CHUNG
does not do maths

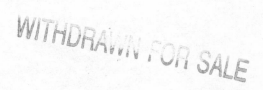

DANNY CHUNG

does not do maths

MAISIE CHAN

illustrated by ANH CAO

Piccadilly
PRESS

First published in Great Britain in 2021 by
PICCADILLY PRESS
80–81 Wimpole St, London W1G 9RE
Owned by Bonnier Books
Sveavägen 56, Stockholm, Sweden
www.piccadillypress.co.uk

ISBN: 978-1-80078-001-9
Also available as an ebook and in audio

1

Typeset by Perfect Bound Ltd
Printed and bound in Great Britain by Clays Ltd, Elcograf S.p.A.

Piccadilly Press is an imprint of Bonnier Books UK
www.bonnierbooks.co.uk

This book is dedicated to the memory
of Jean and Ron – my mum and dad.
And also to the Chan, Kwan and Mui families
who I grew up with and who inspired this book.

1

Half Duck, Half Dragon

Drawing makes me feel good.

I draw literally everywhere: in bed with a torch, and even on the toilet (well, you can be sat for quite a while, and yes, I always wash my hands afterwards). Sometimes I sketch in the park at weekends with Ravi, my best mate. My favourite bit is coming up with new characters; ones that are half one thing and half another – the best of both worlds, like wholemeal bread and white bread put together.

I was really pleased with my newest creation that I called a DRUCKON. It was a mutant duck

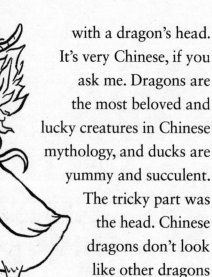

with a dragon's head. It's very Chinese, if you ask me. Dragons are the most beloved and lucky creatures in Chinese mythology, and ducks are yummy and succulent. The tricky part was the head. Chinese dragons don't look like other dragons and they have no wings. Ravi is basically an expert on all things things *medieval* and *knights*. He says that Chinese dragons are anomalies, which is a nice way of saying they're 'weird'. And they don't go around trying to eat princesses or battle knights. I think that's nice. A druckon is a Chinese win-win.

From under my duvet, I heard the door to my room squeak open.

'Danny? Where are you?' It was Ba. I could tell from the sesame-oil smell from the kitchen.

Not now, I prayed – I was still drawing. I

had nearly finished the camel-like head of the dragon. The duck's body would, of course, be in scale with the head. You wouldn't want a tiny duck's body and a massive dragon's head. That thing would lollop around and flop over. I slid my duvet up over my head some more, hoping Ba wouldn't see me. Saturdays were usually very busy, so my parents wanted me to help out by folding menus or piling pop cans on the shelf behind the counter. But I'd rather just draw in my pyjamas instead.

'We can see you, Danny Chung,' Ma's voice said. 'Come on, you need to leave your bedroom now. Ba and I have to clean under your bed – it's like a rubbish tip under there. There has to be more space in here.'

What? I peeked out from under the duvet. Ma had on her red apron that she wore when she did the counter each evening and bright yellow rubber gloves. Under her armpit was the feather duster. She was scanning my bedroom like she was on a mission. Ba knelt down with a pearly-green dustpan and brush. He threw some black bags onto the carpet. Something wasn't right. His head was sweaty and he was all huffy. They never came in here to clean my room.

'Yes, we don't have much time,' Ba said. 'We've been so busy and now we only have a few hours left.' He frantically started dragging out random things that I had shoved under my bedframe. What was going on? A few hours left until what? Ba flung an old teddy bear out from under my bed – it only had one eye. Next, he stretched and pulled out a stack of old sketch books that were filled to the brim with my creations.

'Clean? But it's Saturday. Can't I just relax like the kids at school? On the weekends they play computer games and go for ice cream. Saturdays are for doing . . . I dunno . . . nothing.' Uh-oh. I regretted it as soon as I had uttered the word 'nothing'. I was going to get my dad's Chinese Way lecture.

'Doing . . . nothing? Nothing?' Ba got up from his knees and wiped the dust bunnies and straggled hair from his trouser legs. 'It is not the Chinese Way to do NOTHING, Danny.' Ma lifted her eyebrows at me. She knew what was coming. She started humming a little out-of-tune ditty while her feather duster skimmed the top of my wardrobe.

'The Chinese Way is hard work. It is about listening and respecting our elders. It is about family and helping each other gain success. We have to work doubly hard in this country. Six days a week. No one gives us free things. We don't do . . . NOTHING!' Ba blustered.

'I didn't mean it that way. I meant . . .' What did I mean? 'I just like drawing, that's all. It's not really doing nothing. Look, I'm making something.' I turned my sketch book around so he could see what I was working on. Ma peeked over Ba's shoulder to get a glimpse and squinted her eyes. Her head tilted. She was obviously confused. They swapped places. Ba tutted, then got back down on the floor, and Ma moved in closer to see my picture.

'It's a dragon-and-duck hybrid,' I told her. I hoped she would see how great and Chinese it was. I turned the book back towards me. They didn't get it.

'Oh, okay . . . oh, look, it's Blue Bear!' she said, bending down. She picked up the dirty old bear. It was more grey than blue now. 'I've not seen him for years. He just needs a good wash,' Ma said, brushing off the cobwebs.

'It's kinda disgusting, Ma, and I'm eleven, not two,' I said, wondering why she'd want to keep that ugly thing. 'You can throw it away.'

'How can you say that? Nai Nai sent it for you all the way from China,' said Ma.

'She won't even know it's gone,' I replied. If there was one thing I didn't mind being thrown in the bin, it was that bear. My Chinese grandmother, who I'd never even seen, wouldn't know, so why did I need to keep it?

'She *will* know, Danny . . . I mean . . . she will know that you didn't appreciate her gift,' she said quickly.

Ba shook a black bag open, and grabbed a pile of my old sketch books.

'Ba, wait! Don't throw those away.' My heart beat faster in my chest. I couldn't remember what was in those books, but I knew they deserved a better fate than the recycling bin.

Shaking the the dust from the top of one, he flicked through it. That wasn't a good sign. He stopped at one page and looked at it.

'DANNY CHUNG DOES *NOT* DO MATHS...?
What does that mean? We all do maths –
everybody does maths.' I'd forgotten I had started
that particular comic strip. I'd been bored in class
while Mr Heathfield was talking about long
division and I'd begun to draw all the things
I *could* be doing instead of maths. It included
balancing on a beach ball while playing a trumpet,

blowing paper darts through a straw and flying on a giant kite in the shape of a stingray that had turbo jets underneath.

'Oh, that was just for fun. A joke to make Ravi laugh.' This was not the time to bring up how I had a *hate–hate* relationship with maths. Often I would try to get Ravi to help me or I would just give an excuse to Mr Heathfield if I couldn't do a maths question. He thought I had a dog who ate my homework.

Ba wasn't impressed. 'If you tell yourself you cannot do something, then you will not succeed at it. You need the right mindset. This . . . drawing stuff. It has no purpose.' He put the whole pile of sketch books into the black bag. I felt like my hard work had been truly trashed.

'But I like it,' I mumbled, hugging the book I was now working in.

Ba obviously hadn't heard about famous painters like Van Gogh (all right, he was poor his whole life and had a terrible incident with his ear, but now his paintings were worth millions). I tried to think of a less tragic artist that was famous. I slid my drawings under my pillow.

'But why, Ba? Why can't I be like Picasso?'

'Why do you want to be like a Pika-wossit . . . the yellow squeaky mouse thing from the telly?' He shook his head in confusion. 'That's not a career, Danny.' I wondered if he was imagining, as I was, a grown-up me dressed in a Pikachu onesie, holding a briefcase and going to an office. I stifled a laugh.

'No, Ba, Picasso was a Spanish artist. He said, "Every child is an artist" – he was very famous. He's not a Pokémon.'

Ba sat down on the side of the bed, shuffled next to me, then put his arm around my shoulders and gave me a squeeze.

'Son, for your own good, you should do more constructive things in your spare time. You can draw in art class at school, but after you come home, you need to focus on getting good grades. We don't want you to work in the takeaway like us. Maths, science, English – these are the subjects you have to work on.'

'Your ba is right,' Ma said, pulling bits of fluff from the bear.

Ba looked me straight in the eyes. 'I love you, Danny, but no more drawing, okay?'

He rose and glanced around the room; his

brows furrowed, causing slight wrinkles on his usually smooth forehead. 'Anyway, we have to make room for a new bunk bed. It's arriving in half an hour. Then I need to go and get my –' Ba was about to say something but Ma swatted him on the arm.

She interrupted, 'We need to get a move on . . . get dressed now,' still clutching the blue-grey bear. 'The Yees will be here any moment with the bunk bed.' She glanced at Ba. It was a look that I couldn't understand.

'Give me some privacy and I'll get dressed, okay? I guess that's something to look forward to.' I got out of bed. A new bunk bed was gonna be great because my mattress was sagging in the middle a little.

Ba patted my shoulder; he looked tired. Ma led Ba out of the room with her hand on his waist, and he dragged the black bag behind him like a bad Santa. *Bye, drawings! I shall miss you!* I wanted to shout. I was determined never to be in that position again. From now on I would have to do stealth drawing.

They were whispering about something as they went down the stairs. I could hear Ma telling Ba off. 'Not yet . . .' were the only words I could make out.

Not yet? What was *not yet*?

2

Cyborg Devils of the House of Yee

'We come bearing gifts! Where is Danny?' Auntie Yee boomed.

Auntie Yee's voice was so loud I could hear it upstairs as I pulled my sweatshirt over my head and zipped up my jeans. It was like she needed everyone along the high street to hear what she was saying. I flicked through my sketch book to the drawing I had done last week after Auntie Yee's visit.

CYBORG DEVILS OF THE HOUSE OF YEE!

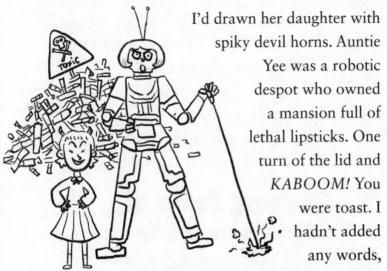

I'd drawn her daughter with spiky devil horns. Auntie Yee was a robotic despot who owned a mansion full of lethal lipsticks. One turn of the lid and *KABOOM!* You were toast. I hadn't added any words, but I would let Ravi fill those bits in when I met him in the park later. He was my comic wingman – he did the speech bubbles to my drawings. I shoved my sketch book into my yellow backpack and hopped downstairs in my slippers.

Like always, Auntie Yee looked like she had just stepped out of a hair salon, and a nail salon, and a ladies' fashion boutique. And behind her was Auntie Yee's mini-me – Amelia Yee. They were always in colour-coordinated outfits, like weird twins. Amelia's brace glinted at me as she forced a half-smile. Being required to hang out with Amelia Yee was basically torture. She didn't want to be here and I didn't want her to be here either. But it was the Chinese Way to act respectful and so we pretended we got on.

Auntie Yee placed her cake tin on the dining table and opened it, revealing yet another steamed cake (if you can call it a cake), which we usually had to force down with buckets of jasmine tea.

'Hi, Auntie Yee,' I said, waving my hand. Just for the record, she wasn't my real aunt. I had to call her auntie because that is also the Chinese Way.

'Thank you so much for bringing the beds!' Ma said, beaming at Amelia. 'You're such a kind girl.'

'You know, anything to help . . .' Amelia said, then turned and whispered so only I could hear her '. . . those less fortunate.' She grinned then added, 'I've got a new double bed with a TV that pops up at the end. A girl at school had one and Mummy said I could have one if I passed my piano exam. I got Grade 3.'

'She's excelling. Those extra lessons we bought are really doing the trick. Three times a week she has a tutor. We're run off our feet taking Amelia to all of her extra-curricular activities. You know how it is, Su Lin!'

'Oh, yes, of course . . . impressive, Amelia,' Ma said. 'Danny, tell Amelia about what you have been doing and about your . . . things.'

'My things?' I asked. I had no clue what she was on about.

'Danny, how is school going?' Auntie Yee inquired. It was the question she always asked when she came. It is also the least interesting subject a child can be interrogated about.

'Danny is doing well at school too,' Ma interjected. 'He's always working so hard. His head is always in a book.' Ma gave me a squeeze and ruffled my hair. Amelia glanced at me and then smirked.

Auntie Yee was always telling my parents I should do this and that. Luckily, we didn't have the money for lots of extra private lessons – my parents were trying to save up to buy a new house.

'Danny, your mother told me you stopped the violin lessons. I suggest you take up the piano instead. The secret is constant practice.' She turned to Ma. 'Invest in your child and your child will invest in you when you are old, as well you know.' My two months of torture last year, also known as violin lessons, were a waste of money and time. Ba was the one who begged my mum to stop paying for them. 'The boy isn't talented at all; he sounds like a strangled cat,' I heard him say. Ba was right, it was not my thing. In fact, I played badly on purpose! It was the one time I was glad to be rubbish at something.

Ba wedged the front door of the takeaway open. I could see Uncle Yee taking out long planks of white wood from the back of the van and passing them to Ba to stack outside the window. Ba looked concerned – there were a LOT of pieces of wood. Uncle Yee slapped him on the back and chuckled. He carried a whole mattress all by himself. Ba lifted up a headboard and brought it in; he was already a little breathless. Uncle Yee winked at me as he approached – the mattress in his big arms.

'Hey, little man, how are you doing?' he chimed, his bald head shining under the light. He was the only Yee I could stand.

'I'm fine, thanks,' I replied.

'We'll get this beast up in no time at all. Ready

for when your – owww.' Ba had accidently nudged Uncle Yee with the headboard.

'Sorry, sorry. Couldn't see you there.' Ba gave an impatient look to Ma, as if to say, *Stop the chit-chat*.

'Thanks so much, Adrian,' Ma said. 'We left the chocolates that you like – Ferrero Rocher – on the living-room coffee table, help yourself when you are up there.'

'Oh, my favourites!' said Uncle Yee. He turned and bounded up the stairs with the mattress like it was made of candyfloss. Ba struggled behind with the headboard. I could hear him ricocheting off the walls as he went up.

'Come, let us sit and have some snacks,' Ma said, inviting Auntie Yee and Amelia to sit at our dining table. It was behind the counter and had been laid out with jasmine tea and a tin of egg rolls. A small fruit bowl sat in the middle. Auntie Yee sat and indicated to Amelia to sit down next to her. Amelia took her furry rainbow backpack off and plonked it on the table. Everyone was trying to avoid the jaundiced sponge cake.

'Bag off the table, Amelia, we're not ruffians,' said Auntie Yee. She'd been talking all 'posh' since being booted out of the Women's Society, which, according to Ba, was some kind of women's club in a nearby county where they baked a lot of cakes. Her steamed Chinese sponges were not a resounding success, so instead she liked to bring them here. Ma usually told me to take them to the park to share with Ravi, if like today, no one was brave enough or stupid enough to eat any. We often played Frisbee with them and then scooped the bits up and plopped them in the bin, as we didn't want to poison the wildlife.

Amelia grabbed her bag and shoved it on the floor near her feet. Then she got out her tablet and started to swipe left and right.

'So, are you looking forward to having bunk beds, Danny?' asked Auntie Yee.

'Yes, I can't wait. I am going to invite my best friend Ravi over for sleepovers; I'm seeing him later at the park.' Ma shifted in her seat. She liked Ravi. I didn't think she would disapprove of him staying over, and, in any case, she and Ba worked nearly every evening, so I was alone upstairs. Ravi could keep me company and we could hang out. It would be great to have someone to talk to when my parents were working.

'Amelia never used the top bunk – it was pointless having it to be honest. Adrian thought it would be good for friends staying, but Amelia is too busy for those kinds of things – even weekends are full.' Amelia suddenly looked strange for an instant, and then took a deep breath in. I thought she was really popular at that fancy girls' school her parents paid for, but maybe she wasn't.

'I'm happy it's gone. Sleepovers are immature,' Amelia mumbled. She looked up at us all for a moment, then went back to focusing on her screen. Ma poured the tea.

I sat there wondering what I should do. When Uncle Yee visited, he usually liked to play cards and he'd often give me his spare change. But he was busy with Ba, sorting out the bed. I picked up a sweet egg roll and started munching it. The yellow flakes fluttered onto my lap. I wiped my hands on my trousers. Then slid on my trainers, which were kept at the bottom of the stairs. Ravi would be waiting in our spot at the park, and any excuse not to listen to Auntie Yee comparing me to Amelia was worth going out for. Amelia and Auntie Yee. **CYBORG DEVILS**, both of them, bashing whole villages with their handbags of destruction. Their sonic singing would shatter even the strongest windows.

'Su Lin, has Danny told you about the maths competition that all of the schools in the area are entering? Amelia is sure to win, as she's been working on it for six weeks now.' Amelia's face went bright red. 'While other children frivolously play in parks . . .' Auntie Yee looked at me, 'my Amelia has been working tirelessly on her presentation skills.' I bit my bottom lip. My class had been nominated to represent the school in the city-wide competition called Maths Is Fun too. Oh God, we didn't stand a chance against Amelia *aren't-I-ever-so-clever-and-good-at-everything* Yee. It would be one more thing for Auntie Yee to lord it over my ma with. Brilliant. Not.

'Danny, you mentioned your class is also taking part, right?' said Ma. Great. Just what I didn't want Auntie Yee to know.

'Yep.' I looked down, waiting for it . . .

'Yes, well, Danny, good luck, but you're up against really strong competitors from our school. You know, because it's a private school. Smaller class sizes and all that. But I'm sure your school is totally fine too.' Auntie Yee picked up her tea and sipped it, her pinkie finger stuck out to the side like it was begging to be away from her. Ma picked up her mug that said 'KEEP CALM AND CARRY ON' and gulped down some tea.

'Mummy, I want to go home. I've got a headache.' Amelia gathered her tablet and jacket and put them into her bag. Ma was confused, as was Auntie Yee, who was most put out – this was her only adult social activity of the week. Being the only two Chinese families within five miles of each other had made my mum and Auntie Yee like magnets. They stuck together but were opposites in many ways.

'But, darling, your father is still assembling the bed,' Auntie Yee called out as Amelia walked towards the front door.

'I want to go,' she repeated.

'Can I do anything?' Ma said. She got up, worry plastered on her face. She didn't want to upset her only friend. 'Was it something that you ate?' I knew that Amelia hadn't touched a thing. It was something else.

'I'm sorry, Su Lin, we'll all have to go. I'm sure you can figure out the bed yourselves.' Auntie Yee trotted over to the stairs and called up: 'Adrian, we have to go! Amelia has an issue. Adrian. NOW!'

Uncle Yee's feet thudding down the stairs made our TV rattle. He appeared flustered. 'What? We need to go? But I haven't got the frame sorted yet,' he said, munching on a Ferrero Rocher.

'I'm sure it will be fine. Danny can help. Come on now.' She tugged at Uncle Yee's rolled-up sleeve. He shrugged and held his hands up in defeat.

'Sorry, Danny. I hope the bed is up for your big surprise.' Uncle Yee patted me on the back. Ba's feet were jogging down the stairs.

Auntie Yee had almost made it to the front door. 'Amelia, darling, we are coming! Su Lin, I'll see you in a couple of weeks, and then we can go out for dim sum when the kids are off for Easter, okay? Call me.' Auntie Yee yanked Uncle Yee out of the takeaway.

'What IS this surprise, Ma?' I asked. She turned to me and put the whole steamed cake into a paper bag so I could take it to the park as a snack.

'Who will be surprised?' said Ba, joining in the conversation, beads of sweat running down his face.

'You,' she said to him. 'The surprise is that we

have to build the beds ourselves because the Yees have left. And we've only got two hours to do it before you are due to get the "surprise".' Ma used her fingers in air quotes when she said 'surprise' and raised her eyebrows at Ba.

'Why isn't anyone telling me what's going on? What is my surprise?' I repeated, bouncing up and down on my toes.

'Ahh, Danny, we don't often get you surprises, so we want to make sure it's a special occasion.' Ma had tears welling up in her eyes.

Ba put his arm around my shoulder. 'Danny, just go out and play at the park, okay? Be home by four and then you will see. You will love it!' I felt butterflies in my stomach. I grinned at them both. It wasn't my birthday, nor was it Chinese New Year, and here I was getting bunk beds AND another surprise! They didn't have to tell me twice to scarper.

3

Sir Ravi of Longdale

There wasn't much to do in my neighbourhood apart from go to the park. It was less than fifteen minutes down the road from where our takeaway, Lucky Dragon, was on the high street. At the weekends I would meet Ravi by the bench near the playground. That day, he was already sitting on it reading a comic when I arrived.

'Hey! What's up?' Ravi said. He was wearing new bright-white trainers with a red tick on the side. I was wearing his old black ones from a couple of years ago. I was an average-sized kid for my age, but Ravi was already wearing clothes for fourteen-year-olds. He could be a basketball player if he wanted to be – except he was rubbish at catching. And throwing. And hated running.

'Your trainers are so bright they can probably see you from Mars,' I chuckled. 'Hey, guess what?' I sat down next to him and opened my backpack (another Ravi hand-me-down).

He pushed up his glasses and frowned, putting down his comic on the bench. 'Errr . . . Mr Heathfield has taken the year off and we won't have to do that maths "thing" he's been talking about and embarrass ourselves in front of the whole class.'

'If only. That would have been nice, but no . . . You, my oldest and most esteemed friend, can now come for sleepovers!' I poked him in the ribs with my finger lance multiple times. It was more like a tickle-poke. He jiggled out of the way.

'Stop it!' Ravi laughed. 'But where would I sleep? Your room is *titchy* tiny. I don't do floors.

Our house might be overcrowded, but I ain't no peasant.'

'This morning the Yees, instead of giving me indigestion or a headache, brought over a bunk bed! My parents are making it as we speak. Dad was a bit stressed because the Yees basically dumped it and left him to it.'

'A sleepover would be amazing – I need just one night away from Vishal's stinky backside. I tell you, Mum should stop giving him eggs. Every time he eats eggs . . . our bedroom smells like a compost bin with a fart machine trapped inside. You're lucky you're an only child. My house is always full of people. I can't think sometimes.'

'Ah, but at least you have a games room you can escape to, and a garden.'

'Yeah, but I can't sleep there, can I?' Ravi grinned at me, hopeful.

'Our flat's sometimes a bit boring though. We never play any games. And my parents say they want me to do well at school, but they don't have time to help me with my homework.'

'My parents don't do that either. Dad's always working and Mum's sorting out Vishal or trying to stop my sisters from failing their exams. You can do what you want at home. No one's under your feet because they're always in the kitchen.'

'Well, I'm just saying, it can get a bit . . . you know . . . quiet . . . Not that I'm lonely or anything.'

Carter and Mitchell from our class appeared from the playing field adjacent to the park and ran towards the playground, blaster guns held across their chests. They charged across dirt-filled flower beds that had no flowers in them. Carter hit Mitchell with the navy-and-yellow foam pellets, and they weaved in and out of the hedges. Jay Jay, the smallest of their gang, was in the bushes. They didn't notice us, or if they did, just ignored us.

I turned back to Ravi.

'Want some Frisbee cake?' I asked, lifting up Auntie Yee's sponge.

'No, thanks,' he replied, eyeing Carter and his crew. 'Do you think we should move away from them?' Ravi asked me, as his foot began to tap nervously on the floor.

'I think we're okay. It's a big park and it's not like they'd ever ask us to play with them.' Although secretly, I would've really liked to play

Blaster Hide and Seek – Carter said he invented it. He and his gang talked about it all the time at school and it looked so much fun. But as I said, they never asked us and Ravi disliked Carter, so it was never going to happen.

I sneaked a peek at Carter's blaster. It was one of the automatic ones I'd seen on the telly! It was a limited edition! They even had walkie-talkies. Cool. Ravi broke my staring with a poke in the ribs. We liked to call them 'finger-jousts' because it sounded medieval.

'Oi! Hello? Earth calling Sir Danny.'

'Sorry? What?' I didn't want to upset Ravi, but, man, I wished he'd be a bit more like the knights he loved so much – you know, running around on quests and missions. He preferred to read about them instead.

'Do you want to do the speech bubbles for the Cyborg Devils?' I asked.

'Does a duck swim in water? Yeah, of course I do. Pass it here.' Ravi held out his hand.

I opened up my sketch book. The **CYBORG DEVILS** section took up a lot of the front of the book. Later in the comic, Amelia had morphed into a Transformer with a metal grille

for a mouth and spiky diamonds of death coming out of her shoulder pads. Her mother had become a mechanical poodle mixed with a wrestler. Ravi laughed when I showed him. Then I remembered what I had drawn that morning.

'Oh, hang on . . . look, I think you will appreciate this,' I said, and opened the page to the druckon. 'It's a dragon mutant duck.' I handed it to Ravi. He studied the page and began nodding his head, chuckling to himself.

'Yeah, yeah, it's fierce. I love it. **THE DEADLY DRUCKON OF LONGDALE** . . . ohh, ohh, can I add something?' I passed him a pencil from my bag. He began to scribble in his tiny handwriting.

'Oww, what was that?' Ravi said, rubbing the back of his head. He turned slowly. I could see Carter, Mitchell and Jay Jay coming towards us.

29

I looked at Ravi. He raised his eyebrows.

'Just when you're having fun, they show up,' Ravi said. He and Carter used to be friends in nursery. But Carter had dumped him on the first day of primary school to hang out with Jay Jay and Mitchell. Ravi had never forgotten it. Carter often ignored Ravi like he didn't exist.

'That's mine,' a familiar voice said. Carter was shorter than both Ravi and I, but his gelled up hair made him seem big. He had a sprinkle of facial hair appearing above his lip and his chest was double the size of ours. Carter was solid despite being in the same year. He held his blaster across his chest with two hands like a Storm Trooper on a mission. Mitchell and Jay Jay were jogging behind him grinning like hyenas.

'Is this the Knights of the Round LOSER Table or whatever it is you two like to play?' Mitchell asked.

'Ha ha, yeah, remember they do that poking thing at school!' Jay Jay said, jabbing his finger into Mitchell's armpit. Mitchell was laughing his head off, trying to stab his finger into Jay Jay's side.

'It's finger-jousting, knucklehead,' Ravi mumbled under his breath.

His shoulders hunched and he closed the sketch book that was on his lap and dropped it into my bag. They were always saying stuff about Ravi's love of knights. He knew it was best if they didn't see the stuff we had drawn.

'Oh, hi, Carter,' I said. I bent down to pick up the pellet that had hit Ravi and stood up tall.

'I like your blaster. That one's really cool. I saw it on TV.' And I *did* really like his blaster; I wasn't just saying that so I wouldn't get shot in the head with a foam pellet like Ravi had. I heard a small sigh from my best friend.

'Yeah, my dad bought it for me last weekend,' Carter said. He was wearing khaki combat trousers and had black stripes on his face. Rumour had it that Carter's dad bought him anything he wanted because he'd got a new family and felt guilty about leaving Carter and his mum. Mitchell and Jay Jay had Blasters and black stripes on their faces too.

'Shame your aim is so bad,' mumbled Ravi, leaning his elbows on his knees.

'I think his aim was pretty good,' jeered Jay Jay.

I had a flashback to World Book Day in infants when Mitchell had thrown Ravi's knight's sword onto the roof of the bike shed. I wondered if I could do anything to dampen the tension and make these guys go away. Carter just stood there and laughed. I really couldn't believe he and Ravi had once been friends.

'Hey, Carter, I have a rubbery sponge cake you can have if you want. It can be like one of those clay pigeon things you shoot.' I grabbed my bag and handed him Auntie Yee's steamed failure. 'You can throw it into the air and try to hit it.'

Carter took the yellow disc, passing it to Jay Jay, who threw it high into the sky. 'All right, laters, we're out of here, geeks!' shouted Mitchell. Carter ran off, blaster aimed at the sky, trying to hit Auntie Yee's inedible sponge. They were always calling us 'geeks', but geeks were clever. And we weren't that smart. The label just didn't fit.

'See ya, wouldn't wanna be ya!' shouted Jay Jay, jogging off with blaster in hand. I watched as the three of them ran around trying to hit the yellow disc. It kinda looked like it would be fun.

Jay Jay and Mitchell were the ones who always said stuff to us, which made me think that Carter wasn't so bad. But Ravi said, 'Birds of a feather flock together.'

'Carter thinks he's in the actual army!' I whispered. Ravi forced a laugh but was still rubbing the back of his head. 'I like that blaster he has. I wonder how much they cost,' I said. 'Maybe we should get some? They might let us play if we had the right stuff. If we show them that we aren't geeks.'

'Looks a load of rubbish, if you ask me,' Ravi grumbled.

'Yeah, probably . . . probably a load of rubbish, as you say.'

'There are too many wannabe soldiers around here for my liking,' Ravi said.

I knew when Ravi got like this I had to change the subject fast. 'Hey, can you help me come up with the words for my druckon?'

'Sure,' said Ravi. He was being quiet. A bit of comic-creating might cheer him up, I thought. He began to write. I glanced over as the pencil scribbled some words.

DOWN WITH WARLORDS!

The druckon was hit in the head by the evil warlord's catapulted rock. The druckon had a small headache but knew he had to get revenge. He flew high over the green pastures searching for the fiend.

We spent hours working on a whole storyline. The druckon devoured the henchmen (henchmen always die in films) and the evil warlord begged forgiveness, giving up his catapult forever. It was ace. Ravi even said the druckon could lay eggs at the end and have an army of his own. A baby druckon army! That's why me and Ravi made a good team. He always came up with great ideas.

After we'd finished, I packed up my pencil case and sketch book.

'Wanna come back to my place for a bit?' Ravi rolled up his comic and slid it into his inside jacket pocket.

'Can't. My dad's bringing me some kind of surprise.'

'But it's not your birthday until next January,' Ravi said. 'That's months away.' He always remembered my birthday and my phone number off my heart, mainly because we were the only kids in our year who didn't have mobile phones yet. Tia, from school, calls us 'retro'.

'I know. I can't wait to see what it is!'

'Well, let me know what you get at school on Monday and we can start planning the bestest, fiercest sleepover ever.' Ravi stood up.

'I will. See ya, Sir Ravi,' I said, jabbing him in the ribs with my index finger.

4

THIS Is My Surprise?

The takeaway smelled like incense when I returned. The wooden altar on the wall where my parents prayed to the Kitchen God was full of offerings and lit joss sticks. The smoke wafted around in swirls of grey. Some large red-and-white laundry bags were leaning against the counter. I peeked inside to see if there was a cool thing for me in there – perhaps a blaster or games console – but there were only clothes. I heard muffled noises and footsteps walking about in our flat above.

I quickly took my trainers off and galloped up. 'Ma? Ba?' I called out as I pounded up the stairs.

Ba stood by my bedroom, filling the door frame with his body. Trying to peer around him wasn't working; he sidestepped, blocking me more. The plastic boxes that had always been in the corner of my room were now out on the landing.

'Wait a minute, Danny,' Ba said. He was beaming.

'Hi, Danny, we've finished making the bed,' said Ma behind him. 'We're so relieved – it was easier than it looked.'

I had a warm squiggly feeling in my belly. The anticipation was eating me alive.

'Ah, Ba! Let me in!' I bobbed my head to one side.

'You're going to be so happy,' Ma said, peeking her head out from under my dad's armpit. She was grinning from ear to ear. I hadn't seen her smile like that for ages.

'Danny, it's going to be different and you will have to adjust, but it will be so great for you to have links to your roots now,' Ba said.

Roots? What was Ba going on about? Had they done a sixty-minute makeover on my bedroom like they did on TV? I'd wanted some cool bean bags, and matching duvets. I heard a cough. Someone else was in my room. Was it Uncle Yee again? Had he come back to help?

'Close your eyes,' Ba said. He put his warm hands around my eyes and I edged forward like a blind zombie, one wobbly step at a time.

'It is so exciting! Come, come,' said Ma. Ba moved his hands away. I blinked, eagerly searching for something that resembled a gift. The room looked exactly the same as it had in the morning: the wallpaper still had ugly cerise flowers on it; the curtains were a dull grey. I felt disappointed that the walls hadn't been painted over. Nothing seemed that different apart from the towering white bunk bed, which looked awesome, and a little old lady who sat on the lower bunk.

A little old lady who had the same nose as my dad.

She had grey hair fashioned into a short bob and was wearing a headband. She also wore a baggy purple cardigan that had

two pockets; they bulged as if they were full. Her feet dangled precariously like a toddler's. She stood up and moved towards me with her arms outstretched. As her mouth opened into a grin, I noticed that a couple of her top teeth were gold, like a pirate's; the rest were slightly yellow.

The strange old woman scuttled closer and took hold of me around my waist. I glanced down to see her face. Her wrinkles smiled when she did.

'Why-is-she-in-my-room?' I asked, breathing heavily. I craned my neck to look at my parents. They stood, holding one another's hands. What was going on? They never held hands.

'She's my mother, Danny – your nai nai. She's come to live with us.' Ba came towards us. I felt like prey being squeezed by a python. Nai Nai? She was here? In Longdale?

Ba crouched down and put his arm around the stranger – I was now encased in a multiple hug. I glanced over to Ma and her eyes were welling with tears. I felt like I could cry too, but obviously for other reasons. The old woman let me go. It slowly dawned on me why I had a bunk bed.

No . . . it *had* to be a joke.

Bunk bed.

Little old lady from China who looked like my dad?

NO WAY!

My face must have been contorted into a frown because Ba came over, leaned in towards me and said through gritted teeth: 'Danny, we have to respect our elders. Give Nai Nai a hug . . .' He pushed my back. 'She has been waiting for you to get back so she could finally meet you in the flesh.' He said it in his *I'm-not-really-asking-you* voice.

'She wants to hold you and tell you how much she loves you. We've been planning this big surprise for you for months,' Ma added.

Nai Nai started chattering to me in sounds I didn't recognise. It only vaguely sounded like the Cantonese that my parents spoke to each other, of which I only knew a few words like 'egg' and 'cat', which would not get me very far in any conversation. Of course Amelia attended the Chinese school in the city and was already fluent in both Cantonese and Mandarin.

Nai Nai sounded like a mixture between a

baby singing and a frog. She took my hand and patted it with hers. The skin on her fingers was dry, but her hands were warm.

'Why's she talking like that?' I asked. She moved forward and grabbed my face. Holding both my cheeks between her thumb and index fingers, she began wiggling them forward and back, pinching the fat in her fingers.

'It's Mandarin Chinese mixed with her local dialect. She lived in an area where they spoke this language. She had her own store. She's very smart,' said Ba.

Nai Nai pulled me close to her again, this time resting her head on my chest, and squeezed me again. There was a lot of squeezing going on. I'm not a boy who likes hugs. Maybe I could teach her to finger-joust rather than doing the *huggy* thing?

'She's squeezing me . . . too much . . .' I gasped. For someone so small, she was very strong.

Nai Nai let go and gave me a big wet kiss on the cheek. I rubbed it off with the back of my hand and wiped it on the side of my top.

'Has she always been this small or has she shrunk?' I asked, eyeing her up for size. She went over to a bag on the floor.

'Yes, she's always been small. She used to joke that she was small and mighty like an ant,' said Ba.

ANT GRAN – I could see a comic strip forming in my mind. Half-ant, half-geriatric warlord. The evil Ant Gran, pulling in prey with her antennae filled with poison. I watched her bending down, looking for something. She rummaged around and plucked out a package – it was book-shaped. She held it out to me using two hands, like a tray.

'Nai Nai got you a present,' Ma said.

'Look pleased, Danny,' said Ba. It was easy to see he was concerned about how I was going to behave around his mother, so I politely took the gift and nodded my head.

Nai Nai smiled. She let go of the flat package wrapped in festive snowman paper.

'But it's not Christmas,' I said.

'Just take it and smile, Danny.' Ma did the *don't-be-ungrateful* look.

Gingerly, I picked at the sticky tape on the back. As I unwrapped it, I saw music notes and then a picture of a violin.

'She has the memory of an elephant,' said Ma. 'I wrote to her last year about you starting violin lessons. I haven't had time to update her. Don't worry, we'll give it to Amelia and Nai Nai won't notice that you don't have a violin or any musical talent.' Ma was serious. Saying I had no musical talent, even though it was true, still hurt my feelings. I put the book on the lower bunk and noticed that my football duvet was there and the old ugly bear that had been washed and tumbled-dried now sat on my pillow. Its fur was sticking up like it had been electrocuted. Oh no. That meant . . .

As if reading my mind, Nai Nai trotted over to the bunk bed and began to climb the ladder. She went up halfway and pulled down a handbag. Not only would I have to share my room with her, but she had taken the coolest bed. My duvet had been relegated – no, *I* had been relegated – to the bottom bunk and I'd have to sleep with that bear. And a wrinkly old lady.

'I was going to sleep up there,' I said halfheartedly, knowing there was going to be little I could do about it. In Chinese culture, the older you are, the more say you had. I had the smallest voice in the family. Woe is me, I thought.

Ba said, 'She wanted to be closer to heaven up there.' His face was finally relaxed. He actually looked happy.

Nai Nai came down and rummaged in her handbag. She extracted a maroon-and-white-striped knitted bobble hat and, as if my humiliation couldn't get any worse, she put it on my head and pulled it down over my ears. It took all of my energy not to roll my eyes. My back stiffened and my shoulders began to reach up to my ears. I felt so uncomfortable in it. It felt like a million centipedes were crawling all over my head.

'Well?' said Ma, folding up some clothes and putting them into the chest of drawers. 'You don't look that excited to have met your grandmother. You always wished we had a bigger family. Now we do.' She closed the drawer a little too hard.

I, Danny Chung, had to tread carefully now. I didn't want to trigger the second Chinese Way lecture of the day. 'It's not what I was expecting . . . you know, as a surprise, that's all. I was really excited about Ravi coming for sleepovers, but now he can't.'

'But it's your Nai Nai. Your flesh and blood. She was so happy to see you still had Blue Bear. I told you she would remember him.'

Nai Nai gave me one more kiss on the cheek and then climbed the ladder. She pulled the orange embroidered duvet over her tiny body and within two minutes was snoring. Her snores sounded like a whistle. It was only four-thirty in the afternoon.

'Why is she going to bed already?' I asked.

'Jet lag. She's exhausted from her trip. She'll get up for dinner,' Ba said. 'Come on, let's go out so she can rest.'

We all tiptoed out of my bedroom and congregated in the living room across the landing. Ma closed the door.

'Are you all right, Danny? You look . . . a bit . . . pale,' she said, putting her hand on my forehead.

'I'm okay,' I said, waving her hand off. 'It's just . . .' I didn't know if I should tell the truth or make up something that they'd want to hear.

I decided to try the truth. 'Ba, I was wondering, why now? Why is Nai Nai coming to live with us? Why not when we get a bigger house? Then at least she could have her own room.'

'Oh, Danny, saving money for our house will take a few more years, and Nai Nai was all alone in China. When Ye Ye died three years ago, I wanted to bring her here to live with us, but there has been a lot of paperwork involved.'

'Oh.'

Ma sat on the edge of the sofa and began to stroke my hair. 'We thought you would love having this surprise. Now you won't be all alone up here while we work.'

'Couldn't she stay in the living room on the sofa? I don't get why she has to share my room.'

'It won't be forever, just a few years.' Ba was looking at me like perhaps I wasn't going to be the best grandson in the world.

A few years? I'd be fourteen and still be sharing a room with my gran. Imagine if everyone knew. What about when I went to secondary school? I wanted to curl up and disintegrate into a thousand pieces.

'We've got to get back to the kitchen now. We'll

have dinner together in a bit and I can translate for you. Even your ma doesn't understand everything Nai Nai says.' Ba looked tired.

'Tomorrow we'll show her around. She wants to see where you go to school and wants to spend time with you,' Ma said, rubbing my back. Then they left me.

I was stuck. I didn't want to go downstairs and I couldn't go to my room. I turned on the TV and slumped on the sofa.

Nai Nai didn't wake up for dinner; she kept snoring into the night. The whistling snore escalated into a full rhino-charging sound. Not just one rhino. A herd.

It took me ages to get to sleep that night. It got so bad that I balled up toilet paper and stuck it into my ears, then tried to block out her noise with that itchy bobble hat she had brought for me. My room just didn't feel right any more.

5

Mr Potempa's Global Mini Mart

My eyes were cemented together as I dreamed about a witch-like creature. She was following me along dark corridors, her bony finger outstretched with a glob of smelly menthol stuff on it. Running was my only option. *Get away!* I shouted. *Get away!* I kicked

and punched. I felt tapping on my arm.

Groggily, I opened my eyes and wiped the crusts of sleep away. The bobble hat was still fitted snugly on my head and the wads of tissue were still balled up in my ears. I blinked.

'Arrhhhhhghhh!' I screamed. She was right in front of me! Nai Nai's whole face was slathered in a chalky green paste that was cracking as she grinned. The smell of Tiger Balm was making my eyes water. She was all over me like a sniffer dog.

'Ah, Dan,' she said as she lowered her ear next to my nose. I was SO freaked out. I held my breath and felt my body go rigid like a surfboard. All I wanted to do was jump out of bed and run for it. I had to breathe out as I was bursting. My mouth formed a half-smile. I grimaced. My hand appeared from under the duvet and gave her a little wave.

She grinned back at me. She touched my forehead.

'Zaooooo,' she said with a funny drawl. She gently took off the bobble hat. Then she waddled out of the room. I heard the bathroom door lock.

I sprang out of bed and grabbed some clothes from the floor and a pair of clean pants. I would have to speed-dress before she came back. Is this how I would have to get dressed from now on? I opened my bedroom door and peeked out. I could hear her making some high-pitched, out-of-tune noises.

Ba appeared on the landing in his dressing gown.

'Morning, Danny. I see my mother still likes to sing opera. Did you and Nai Nai sleep well?'

'She slept well. I didn't. It took me ages to get to sleep. She snores, you know! I had to wear that ugly bobble hat over my ears to muffle the sound.'

'Ha ha, yes, my father said he was the only man who could sleep next to such a noise. You'll get used to it. People sleep next to train tracks and after a while they don't hear the trains going past. It'll be like that.' I doubted it very much – the Nai Nai locomotive was loud.

'Ba, Nai Nai was hovering over me this morning. She was by my bed, and her face . . . it was all green! She was touching my head like a nurse and then put her ear by my nose,' I said.

My dad laughed. 'She must have thought you had caught a cold and that was why you were

50

wearing a hat in bed. She was just doing a health check.'

I held up my fingers. 'Seriously, she was this close to my face!'

'Ah, don't worry about it. She was checking that you were still breathing. She used to do it to me too, when I was little.'

'But I'm not a baby, Ba.'

'Yes, but she never saw you as a baby, so she's making up for lost time,' Ba said jokingly.

'Weird, totally weird,' I said. My ancient grandmother was performing baby health checks on me, and my dad was totally fine with that. I'd never heard of anything so silly.

'Don't worry. Once she's satisfied you are healthy, she will stop doing it,' Ba said. 'She just loves you so much and wants to take care of you. It is the Chinese Way, I told you. Grandparents there look after their grandkids a lot. Family is the most important thing.'

'I thought she was trying to kill me!' I said.

'Don't be silly. If she wanted to kill you, she'd do it when you were asleep!' Ba said, laughing. Ma sniggered too, as she appeared on the landing next to Ba. She nudged him with her elbow.

51

'Don't scare him,' she said. 'Come on, let's have breakfast and then we'll take her out for a walk.' They went into their bedroom and shut the door.

I made my way down to the dining table. Nai Nai appeared with her newly washed face and sat down, pulling her chair closer to mine. She poured herself some hot water from the flask. Then poured me some. Ba appeared with Yorkshire pudding, congee and some steamed broccoli. Nai Nai rubbed her hands together, then grabbed my cheeks and gave them a pinch.

'Mmm, yeah, fantastic,' I groaned as Nai Nai began ladling more and more congee into my bowl. I waved my hands over it, hoping to get her to stop. 'Thanks . . . er . . . no more . . . too much. Thanks.' Then she gave herself about a quarter of the amount she had given to me and used her chopsticks to drop broccoli into the middle of my bowl. The florets bobbed there like a mini island surrounded by a white sea. I looked around. This was my family now.

'So, the plan for this morning: we'll walk around the neighbourhood – she wants to see where you go to school – and then Ma and I have to come back to work, but you can show her Mr Potempa's shop. It's good that everything is within walking distance,' Ba said.

'Let's show her the park so she can see the daffodils before they die. Plus, it's the nicest part of Longdale.'

'They already took those out; the flower beds are empty,' I said, recalling yesterday's encounter with Carter trudging through the muddy, flowerless heaps of soil.

'That's a shame,' Ma said as she picked up another piece of broccoli from the serving plate and also dropped it into my bowl. Why was everyone dropping green stuff into my bowl?

I reluctantly crunched on the steamed vegetables.

'Ba, why didn't I ever get to meet Nai Nai before yesterday?' I asked.

'Not now, Danny, just have your food,' Ba said, looking down into his congee.

I held a Yorkshire pudding between my chopsticks. 'But it's weird. Why can't you tell me?' Nai Nai was also munching on one but was using her hands and licking her fingers after each bite.

Ma put her chopsticks down and looked from my dad to me. 'The short version is that your ba and Ye Ye didn't always get along. They didn't have the same ideas about things or life.' That sounds familiar, I thought.

'Why not?' I probed.

Ba huffed, then said, 'Families are complicated, Danny. I didn't speak to him for a long time. But Nai Nai and I would speak on the phone once every few months and I would tell her all about you. I didn't get to talk things through with my father before he died.' Ba's eyes welled up.

'And I would send her photos and a letter every so often,' Ma added. 'But enough of that sad stuff. We have Nai Nai here now. Eat up.'

We walked Nai Nai around Longdale, one of Birmingham's remotest suburbs. There was hardly anyone around on the high street. Ma linked arms with her and Ba strode ahead, pointing at shop windows and talking in the same dialect as Nai Nai. The sausage-roll shop was closed. I wondered if they had sausage rolls in China. We turned the corner, along Fairley Road and down past the park.

We walked her to my school: Longdale Primary. The gates had been painted postbox red last year. Nai Nai looked through the bars and said something to my dad.

'She's saying . . . it looks very auspicious. She thinks it looks like a welcoming place.' Ba, animated now, began talking very fast to his mum. She was nodding and grinning. What were they talking about? Ma put her arms around my shoulders and started saying stuff to Nai Nai too. I couldn't catch any familiar words. 'I've just told her how happy you are here. Best in your class.'

'Maaaaa,' I groaned. 'You don't have to do that. I'm not the best.'

Nai Nai turned and hugged me tightly. She held my face and grinned at me; I did my best to smile.

'Danny, Ba and I need to head back to start the prep for tonight. Can you take Nai Nai to Mr Potempa's? She needs some fruit to help her to be . . . more regular. You know what I mean, right?'

'Of course I know. I'm eleven,' I said.

'Yes, exactly. Great, we'll see you at home.' Ba handed me a shopping bag, then he and Ma said their goodbyes and left me to walk Nai Nai to the grocery store.

Nai Nai tried to walk very close to me, but I sped ahead and didn't say a word. We arrived at Mr Potempa's Global Mini Mart. Mr Potempa was a large man with a thick grey moustache that covered the top of his lip and a beard that had grown down past his chin. Sometimes he had bits of food stuck in there. Once I pointed it out to him, and he laughed and said: 'A snack for later!' He and his husband David were cool. David was from Mauritius and worked 'for the council', but that meant nothing to me. They lived above their shop like we did.

'Who's this you've brought with you, Danny?' Mr Potempa asked, rising from his tatty grey swivel chair and placing his latest novel face-down on the countertop. He was always trying to tell Ma she should join the library so she could borrow books to read during the 'quiet times' when no customers came in. He had a good point, but she said she was always too busy to read.

'This is my grandmother. She's just moved in with us.'

'Hello, Danny's grandmother! Welcome!' Mr Potempa said, waving his hand. Nai Nai had rushed off like a kid in a sweet shop. She was squeezing and smelling everything. She even held up a coconut to her ear and shook it. Next she lifted up a watermelon that was the size of a pug, turned it around and sniffed it. Then she proceeded to bang it with her palm.

Poum! Poum! Poum! it went. Was she doing the *knock-knock* to see if there was someone inside? She shook her head. Then put it down, choosing a smaller one and did the banging thing again. I wondered what kind of sound it was supposed to make for her to be satisfied with it. I looked over to Mr Potempa and shrugged my shoulders.

'I dunno what she's doing. Do you?'

'Yes, the Asian women always do that. They think they can hear if it's ripe or not. Tell her my produce is all fresh. Very tasty. No need to slap it like a naughty baby,' he chuckled.

'She needs some fruit for a special reason . . .'
I did a funny wink at him. 'You know, to do
number . . . twos,' I whispered, forgetting that
Nai Nai couldn't understand English anyway.

'Oh, I see. Well, we've got some nice juicy
plums in, also dried apricots on aisle three
next to the prunes. It's stressful coming to live
in a foreign country, never mind doing it at
your grandmother's age – no offence, Danny's
grandmother.' I hadn't really thought about that.

'Here, give her this.' Mr Potempa passed me a
metal basket and I followed Nai Nai around the
store like her servant. She filled it with two Galia
melons, a grapefruit, some
satsumas and three kiwis.
It was getting quite heavy.
Then she ran over to a
crate on the floor next to
the fridges. Inside sat loads
of red spiky balls on branches.

'Hao-a! Hao-!' *Good, good,* she exclaimed.
She was touching the round red balls, running
her finger over the little bumps. Then she ushered
me to come over. I bent down next to her. I heard
Mr Potempa's feet on the floorboards.

'Oh, I see she likes the lychees,' Mr Potempa said.

'Yes, my mum loves them, too. I don't eat them,' I said. 'They're all slimy and gross. I only eat green fruit.'

'You're missing out, Danny.'

Nai Nai held one up to her mouth. 'Chi-a?' she said, looking at me and then at Mr Potempa. Being a translator was not in my job description. But I thought I would give it a try, even with my limited language skills.

'Can she try one?' I asked.

'Of course, go ahead,' Mr Potempa nodded.

'Chi chi,' I told Nai Nai, and put my hands to my lips to show her she could eat one.

'Look, Danny's grandmother. I will give you a very special offer. You can have four kilos of those for only five pounds. It is only for very special customers, you see.'

'She won't understand you,' I said.

Mr Potempa skipped to the counter and picked up a pad and pen. He scribbled something and then came over to Nai Nai. He showed her the numbers. She'd already peeled two lychees and was sucking on them. One in each cheek. She looked like a hamster. A happy hamster.

'Hao-a!' Nai Nai nodded, still eating the white balls. Suddenly, she held out her hand and spat two shiny black seeds into them. It was gross.

I felt a bit uncomfortable being out in public with her. 'Ergh,' I said.

'Okay, Danny's grandmother, put those in here,' said Mr Potempa, holding out a wastepaper basket. She dropped the seeds in and wiped her hands on her cardigan. I could see spit marks on the purple wool. There was no end to the embarrassment. Nai Nai lifted loads of the lychees into the basket. It was now full. We walked over to the counter. I saw Mr Potempa's novel lying there – a romance this week. Sometimes it was whodunnits.

Mr Potempa twirled around a strange vegetable with spikes. 'I've got an offer on limited-edition cauliflowers too, if you are interested.' It was the weirdest-looking vegetable I had ever seen. I heaved the basket onto the counter and Nai Nai excitedly took the cauliflower thing. She was gawping at it with eyes wide. She ran her hand over the top, then held it out for me to do the same. It felt funny. I traced my fingers around its spiky turrets.

'A Romanesco cauliflower. They are one of my bestsellers, but I don't have them in often.'

It was so out of this world. I imagined the spikes as something I could draw for a character – the back of a special turtle or something like that. That would be a fun comic.

'I don't think we can carry ALL of this home,' I said.

Mr Potempa began ringing up Nai Nai's fruit bounty on the till. When she saw the total, she rummaged through her little pink silk purse. Then I saw her look up, calculating if she had enough. She took out the exact money in change and moved the cauliflower back to its home on the counter, ready to entice someone else.

'Not enough cash today? Don't worry, there will be another shipment in a few weeks,' said Mr Potempa, putting the money into the till. He gave me a free lollipop.

I thought it strange that Nai Nai would understand our numerical digits. I was sure the

Chinese had their own way of writing down numbers. I made a note to ask Ma about it. Even though Nai Nai couldn't speak English, it was useful to know she could at least go shopping by herself. Then she could spit her seeds into the bin without me having to watch.

6

Ant Gran, Supervillain

I never thought I would ever say that I was looking forward to being at school, but on this day I was. And there was no way I was going to sit at breakfast with Nai Nai pinching my face and trying to feed me loads of food. How many times do you need to ask a person if they are hungry?

I got up mega early to try to make sure that I wasn't woken by Nai Nai tapping my arm again or hovering over me with her creepy moisturising mask. But she beat me to it. Her bed was empty. And I noticed she had placed Blue Bear next to my school bag. As if I would take that thing to school! I chucked it across the room, then grabbed my sketch book and pencils. I made my way to the bathroom and locked the door. With a pencil in one hand and my toothbrush dangling from my mouth, I quickly drew my new nemesis – Ant Gran. She was everywhere. Not cool. I finished brushing my teeth. When I was done I rushed back to my room, put on my uniform and legged it downstairs with my backpack. I put on my shoes so I could scarper before she got hold of me.

Nai Nai was in the customer waiting area in a turquoise velour tracksuit. Her bare feet were tiny, her toenails painted bright red. She was punching the air and making 'ha' sounds. Ma brushed past me and put her finger to her lips.

'Qigong,' Ma said.

'What *gong*?' I whispered.

'She's cultivating her life force – it will help her go to the toilet.'

'Oh.' As long as she wasn't planning on sucking out my life force, that was okay. It was probably working, as she wasn't like any old ladies I had seen around here – she was definitely not doddery.

Ba rounded the corner; he was dressed in a new shirt and smart jumper. Nai Nai had bought him clothes too, it seemed.

'Morning, Danny!' he said. He was full of smiles.

'Morning, Ba.'

'It's a bit cloudy outside,' Ma said, bringing out bowls for breakfast. 'I hope the rain stays away and I hope Nai Nai likes where we live.'

'Well, it's certainly different from where I grew up,' Ba replied. 'It's a lot colder here, for sure. She already commented on the many pale faces. On the drive back from the airport she was looking out of the window, pointing: "There's one. Another one. And another." It was really funny. I said she'd get used to it.' I shoved a can of Tango into my backpack and wondered if I could sneak out some cereal without having to sit down to eat it. Everyone was looking at me. Nai Nai finished her gong thing and came behind the counter and sat down. She said something to Ba. He turned to me. 'She said she is here to look after you because you are kindred dragons.'

'What do you mean, we're dragons?' I asked, trying to make my way towards the front door.

LUCKY DRAGON

'Both born in the year of the dragon,' Ba said.

'Oh, right, yeah.'

'You are both my lucky dragons,' Ba said, smiling at me. He nodded as Nai Nai went on talking. Ba came over to me, tapped on his phone screen and showed me the characteristics of those who are born in the year of the dragon:

DRAGONS ARE FIGHTERS
They are good at arts, politics and education.
They have quick-paced thinking.
They work better in a team.

'See, you two will be a great team,' Ba said. 'Two clever, quick-thinking people . . . my lucky dragons.'

Well, I was good at art. That's the only one that sounded accurate. We were definitely not good as a team. I was nothing like Nai Nai. Speaking of which, she was waving at me to sit by her. That was my cue to leave. I'd grab something to eat from the corner shop near school.

'I've gotta go now,' I said.

'What about breakfast? You don't even have your coat on today,' Ma said, laying out the spoons.

'I'll grab something later.'

'All right,' Ma said. Nai Nai looked confused.

'See ya,' I said as I started to jog towards the door.

'Wait,' Ba said.

'What?'

Ma opened her eyes wide and nodded her head to Nai Nai.

'Huh?'

'Tell her goodbye too. Don't ignore her.'

'BYE BYE, Nai Nai!' I yelled.

'She's old, not deaf, Danny,' Ba said.

Nai Nai raised her hand and waved. Then she waddled to the front door and watched me leave. When I turned around, she was still watching and muttering something. She didn't venture out. A double-decker bus zoomed past her and she ducked back inside. Perhaps the sounds of England were a bit much for my new little grandma from China. Fighting dragons, pah.

*

As I entered the school grounds the vibe was electric. Loads of people from my class were gathered around a newly buzz-cut Carter, who was showing everyone his new mobile phone. He'd given Mitchell his old one. I poked my head into the crowd to see what all the fuss was about.

'*Wow, awesome app.*'

'*Cool haircut, Carter.*'

'*It's totally rad . . .*' – blah blah blah.

I raced over to Ravi, who was waiting for me by the bench on the far side of the playground. It was our spot. He waved to me. He was always at school early because his mum had to zoom over to the nursery to drop off his little brother, then take his sisters to the secondary school, where we'd both be going.

'Hey, Ravi.'

'Hey. You're early today.'

'Yep.' I wasn't sure how to broach the subject of Nai Nai.

Ravi moved his glasses up his nose. 'What was your surprise then?'

I decided to just tell him. 'A Chinese granny.'

'Stop being stupid. What did you really get?'

'I just told you.' It did sound stupid, I have to admit.

'What do you mean? Are you talking in code?'

'My dad's mother has flown all the way from China and landed in my bedroom, on the top bunk to be precise. To live. It's not a joke.'

'No way! You being serious? You're sharing a room with your granny?' Ravi's eyes widened and his mouth was attempting not to smile.

'I wouldn't make up something like that,' I said, scrunching up my face.

Ravi sat back against the wood. 'Man, I'm sorry for your predicament. And for mine, because now I can't come and sleep over.' He looked annoyed for a moment, but then he saw the bright side. 'Did she bring presents? My nani always gets me clothes and DVDs when she comes over from India.'

'She gave me a woolly hat – you know I look like a peanut head when I wear a hat of any kind. Oh, and she gave me a violin book.'

'You don't play the violin.'

'I know.'

'Sorry, man.' Ravi tilted his head in a sympathetic

way. But I could see the amusement in his eyes. 'Your granny . . . from China . . . sheesh, that was not what I was expecting.'

'You don't know the half of it. She follows me about, kisses me and plonks broccoli in my congee. She left footprints on the toilet seat too – I could see them.'

'She stands up for a number two?'

'Technically she squats, but yeah. Plus she snores, really loud.'

'Well, now you know what it feels like for me,' said Ravi.

'Nope, it's not the same – a little brother whose farts smell like boiled eggs isn't the same as sharing your bedroom with an old lady who doesn't speak English.'

I rummaged around in my backpack.

'Here, look at this.' I handed him the rough sketches I'd done in secret at home.

ANT GRAN, SUPERVILLAIN

'I only had a few minutes this morning to do this in the bathroom. What do you think?' Yes, the bathroom would have to become a multi-purpose room from now on. I passed the book to Ravi. He flipped through the pages.

'Ohh, yeah, I like this bit . . .' he said.

'What d'ya think of this?
See this, here? She
hoards fruit until

it goes rotten, then fills up her gamma-ray gun
with the sludge and shoots it at people.' I knew
Ravi would love it, maybe even more than my
last comic.

'Yeah, it's intergalactic cool – nice. Can I do a
speech bubble here?'

'Sure, go ahead,' I said. He was the practical
one and also had a way with words.

He got out a pencil that was from his last
visit to Warwick Castle and started writing in the
speech bubble. His handwriting was teeny tiny
so he didn't go over the lines, and I knew that if
I hated it, I could just rub it out. He wrote: 'I will
snore you to death, puny humans.'

We chuckled. It was pretty funny.

The bell rang. We got off the bench and headed towards the rest of the class, who were lined up near the main entrance.

As usual, Ravi and I went to the back. It was the safest place to be, because Carter and his boys always pushed in at the front. Ravi and I slowed down to let them settle into a line. But Carter stood back. He looked at us.

'*We'll* go at the back today,' he said.

'Fine,' Ravi replied, slouching even more than usual.

We took our places in front of Carter, Mitchell and Jay Jay. I was trying to put my book away when someone grabbed it out of my hand. Mitchell.

'What's this?' He held it in the air.

'Give it back,' I said. My belly was flipping inside.

'Drawing ickle pictures, Chung?' He shook the spine of the book. Mitchell was always trying to do things to impress Carter. I tried to grab it back.

'Mitchell, I think you should give it back to him,' said Ravi. His voice was cracking slightly, like his throat was made of ice that someone had just stepped on with a big boot.

'Make me.'

Carter held up his phone and pointed it in my direction. He was recording. 'Go on, you can fight Mitchell. If you dare – he's a yellow belt in judo,' he said, smirking.

'Yeah, Mitchell, throw him!' added Jay Jay. It sounded painful.

'We don't want to fight,' Ravi said, looming behind me and holding up his palms. I edged to the side, wanting to move behind Ravi. We bumped elbows.

'No, we don't,' I said. 'I just want my book back . . . please.' Ravi nudged me.

I turned to see Mr Heathfield, our teacher, coming out of the main doors; he was heading straight towards us. Just in the nick of time, I thought. I looked at Carter. He was peering over his phone at me. Then he glanced to see where Mr Heathfield was.

'Go fetch it!' said Mitchell as he lobbed the book into the air behind us. It landed in a small wet puddle on the grass that edged around the school. I ran over to get it.

'Danny! Get back into line!' I heard Mr Heathfield shout. I picked up my book. I flicked through it to check it wasn't too messed up. Two pages were really soaked but the back half of the book was okay. **ANT GRAN** was saved. But the **CYBORG DEVILS** comic strip, which was at the beginning of the book, not so much. My drawings of Amelia were all smudged. I tried to wipe the dirt off with my sleeve. As I returned to the line, Mr Heathfield made his way to the back and stood in front of me, arms folded in front of his chest.

'Danny, I don't like having to shout at nine in the morning.'

'But, sir, I –'

'You can sit outside the staff room at lunchtime. No more trouble from you today, got it?'

'Yes, sir.'

I'd never had to stay in during lunch for my behaviour before. It must be Nai Nai – she'd brought bad luck with her from China. So much for being a 'lucky dragon'.

7

Chicken Feet Go Viral

Sitting at the back of maths class with my sketch book out, I started to draw a picture of a castle. Tangled weeds grew high around it. A little figure was leaning out from the tower, calling for help. He was my age. He had my hair and he

held a sign. It said, **'SAVE ME!'** Ant Gran was lurking in the bushes below with her arm held aloft, holding a banana ray gun. 'Danny . . . Danny! . . . Earth calling Daniel Chung.'

'Huh?' Quickly shoving my sketch book under my table, I looked up.

'Please switch on your ears.' Mr Heathfield lifted his hands up near his ears and, fingers splayed, turned imaginary knobs. 'As a reminder, these are the criteria, and here is where you should be in your progress. Your maths presentation is due in after the Easter break.' He continued. 'You should already have come up with your ideas about what you want to present to the class.'

'But, sir, what if the dog eats my work before we return to school? Can I be let off?' Carter thought he was so funny. He nudged Amy, who sat next to him.

'If your dog swallows your homework then you will have two projects to do next term.'

'All right, sir, I was only joking.' Carter slumped down into his seat, smirking.

'So we can talk about anything that's to do with maths?' Grace asked.

'Remember, the title for the project is "MATHS

IS FUN!"' Mr Heathfield moved towards the whiteboard. 'The optimal word here is "fun".'

'What you gonna do?' I whispered to Tia. She only joined the class in September from Nottingham. When I tried to ask her questions to be friendly, she just told me to 'stop asking so many questions'. Mostly she leaned away from me and talked to Grace in pig Latin.

'I've got a brilliant idea, but I'm not going to tell you in case you steal it.' She turned and lifted the cover of her exercise book so I couldn't see what she was writing.

'As a reminder, the winner from the region will be put forward to meet the Mayor of Birmingham, who will offer his personal limo for you and your friends to use for the day. Plus, you will receive tickets to the Knights of Old theme park.' I turned and saw Ravi's face light up. We'd seen the adverts for that place on telly. I'd never been to a theme park before, nor even seen a limo, never mind sat in one, but I knew that I would never win the maths presentation prize, so why bother? And Auntie Yee had said Amelia had been working on hers for ages now. I didn't stand a chance.

Plus, me and numbers didn't go together. Like ice cream and cucumbers. Not that I would ever tell Ba that. I looked at the clock on the wall. Not long until lunchtime. I wondered what Ma and Ba were doing right now. Ma mentioned she was going to try to get Nai Nai a free bus pass. It sounded pretty good, being old; you got to travel for free, received discounts at the hairdressers and you could do things and get away with it (like spit out your fruit seeds). I didn't know if that was an old-person thing or a Chinese thing.

'Danny . . . Danny . . . look.' Ravi was tapping my shoulder with his ruler.

'Stop it.' I just wanted to get through the day as quickly as possible. I was worried that Mr Heathfield would pick on me again.

'Sir . . . there's someone in the playground. Sir,' Grace blurted out, craning her neck at an angle and lifting out of her seat slightly.

'It looks like the queen, sir, but with a suntan,' said Damaris.

'Eyes front and centre, please, class.' Mr

Heathfield was getting agitated; his face was beginning to go red.

'No, sir . . . it's not one of us . . . it's an old . . .' said Tia, pushing her glasses up her nose to see better, '. . . lady?'

Please don't let it be her.

Please don't let it be her.

Please, Fat Buddha, don't let it be her.

'It's a Chinese lady, sir,' giggled Carter.

I sighed. *Perfect.*

Mr Heathfield stomped to the window. 'What in the name – ?' He peered through the glass. All of the class got out of their chairs to see who was roaming around the empty playground in school hours. I rushed over to the window as well. Ravi was beside me. I jostled my way to a space at the front.

Ravi leaned over. 'Is that her? Ant Gran?' he said, pointing.

'Yep,' I said, inching away from the window in case she saw me. We all watched as she peered in through the school office windows. Then she headed towards us. She pressed her face up against the glass of my classroom. Her eyes squinted, trying to get a better look. Why did our school only have one level, like a bungalow? Why, oh why, had Ma insisted that we show Nai Nai where my school was?

What was she doing here? I was already in enough trouble today. I didn't need more.

She spotted me. Her face beamed with a massive smile. She waved.

She started tapping on the glass and then held up a plastic bag with the Lucky Dragon logo printed on it in red. Oh no, she'd brought me food. Ba and Ma shouldn't have let her out of the flat into the wild. What were they thinking?

'Danny, do you know that lady?' Mr Heathfield was more annoyed than usual.

'Yes . . . kinda.'

'You either know her or you don't.'

'Okay, I do know her, sir.' It was hard to admit that I was related to her. 'She's my . . . er, gran.'

Mr Heathfield opened the window slightly. It looked like he was afraid she might jump in if he opened it fully.

'Erm . . . hello, you there . . . can you please go to the office area? Daniel's grandmother. Yes, you.' He pointed to the main door at the other side of the quadrangle. Nai Nai grinned and nodded her head. She waved at me. I felt my insides flip over.

Mr Heathfield closed the window and moved towards me. I rushed back to my chair, unsure what to do.

'Okay, you can go out and ask her what she wants. Also tell her that visiting during class time is very disruptive.'

'I can't, sir.' I reluctantly scraped my chair along the floor and half stood up.

'You can't? Why ever not?' He frowned at me incredulously.

'I can't speak her dialect, sir.' Standing now, I put my hands in my trouser pockets. My face was burning red. I could feel my cheeks flushing hot. Embarrassed was too weak a word for what I was feeling.

'She's from a small place in China. The Chinese they speak there is different, sir.'

'Different? Chinese is Chinese, surely? Now go.' I shrugged. People think there is only one kind of Chinese person, but there are loads of different kinds of Chinese people with their own cuisine and even different ways of speaking.

I tried to block out the rest of the class laughing

and the delighted whispers of 'Nana's boy' that followed me out of the classroom. I headed to the reception area.

As I opened the door to the school, Nai Nai was already standing there in anticipation. She came inside, wrapped her arms around me and started kissing my cheek. She held out the bag. Inside  was a plastic box. I lifted the lid. Inside were tasty browned chicken feet – I loved them. The aroma was making my mouth water. My stomach gurgled. I pushed down the lid to block out the wonderful smells.

'No, Nai Nai, I can't eat this at school. I have school dinners. You need to go home.' I wanted to shoo her away but couldn't. I'd definitely be in trouble with Ba if he heard I'd shoved his mother. I pointed to the exit.

'Chi-a, chi, chi.' She opened the lid again,

urging me to eat. She held up a gnarly brown talon to my lips with her metal chopsticks that she'd produced from her inside pocket.

Torn between devouring it and looking like a fool, I shook my head.

'No, I can't eat this here.' I looked at the door of my classroom; everyone was still gawking through the glass window that looked onto the hallway. Mr Heathfield was writing something on the whiteboard and wasn't paying attention. Most were laughing now as Nai Nai shook the chicken's foot in my face, trying to entice me to eat it. I saw Carter filming it on his mobile. Brilliant.

'Dan Dan, chi.'

I knew the only way to get her to leave was to take the food. I opened my mouth and she jabbed in a succulent piece of chicken foot. She didn't quite get it in properly and my cheek was smeared with chicken feet juice. Nai Nai pushed the talons into my mouth, then licked her fingers and wiped my cheeks with them. I chewed and chewed. Why wouldn't it go down faster?

Swallow, Danny.

Swallow.

I grabbed the box and glowered at her that she should go.

'Hao, hao.' She patted my arm.

I nodded.

Nai Nai looked satisfied that her role as feeder was done. I watched her walk away. Finally, I swallowed.

The home-time bell rang. As I looked out of the window the sky was grey. Sheets of rain cascaded down; not a single sliver of blue remained. It was a fitting end to a miserable day.

Carter had sent the video to Mitchell. Mitchell had then sent it to everybody in the school with a mobile. Great – I had gone viral for being force-fed chicken feet. In the main corridor on the way out, people kept doing flapping chicken arms at me when I walked past them. The inventive ones did the noise, too – *bock, bock, bock!* Ravi and I kept our heads down as we walked out.

BOCK!
BOCK!
BOCK!

'Hey, come over later to brainstorm ideas for maths, okay?' Ravi said. 'Gotta go, my mum's taking Vishal to pre-school karate now.' Ravi jogged off to his mum's car, which was waiting outside the gate. I could tell he was trying to take my mind off being humiliated. He was thoughtful like that.

'Oi, Chung!' a voice boomed. I turned to see Mitchell holding his coat above his head like a tent. Carter was underneath, his perfect hair remaining sheltered from the rain.

'Your girlfriend has come to pick you up! She can't get enough of you!' Mitchell shouted.

I was confused.

'I don't have a girlfriend.' I turned back around to face the gate.

Then I saw her. Not again, I thought.

Nai Nai was standing on top of the red wall near the entrance gate in oversized black wellies – they looked like my mum's. How had she got up there? She was scouring the playground, looking for me, like a ship's mate on a pirate galleon looking out of the crow's nest.

Little did she know that her being here was like me walking a metaphorical plank. Splash goes my street cred again, I thought.

'Dan! Dan!' she called when she spotted me. She started to wave a huge rainbow umbrella at me. She was small but you couldn't miss her. A gust of wind made her wobble slightly.

'Excuse me . . . hello? No climbing on the walls!' said one of the teachers from the main entrance. It was Mrs Brannan, the deputy head. She was rushing forward and flapping her hand as though she was trying to swat a fly.

'Oh, it's okay, emergency over . . . it's an elderly lady. Thank God it's not one of the infants!'

Nai Nai was now running along the top of the wall. I ran over. The nearest exit was full of parents wondering why my grandmother was shouting my name from the top of the wall.

'Dan! Dan! Da-ni-ah!'

'Get down, Nai Nai! Please get down . . . please!' I urged.

'Who's this woman here with?' called Mrs Brannan, trying to be heard above the din of parents picking up their children.

'She's with me, miss! I'm sorry, she couldn't see me properly.'

'Health and safety, Danny. Health and safety.

We are not insured for relatives having accidents on school grounds.' Mrs Brannan waved her arms about like a flight attendant in a bid to get Nai Nai to dismount the wall.

'Sorry, miss.'

Nai Nai expertly strode with precise steps along the wall to the metal gate. She had pretty good balance, as that wall was only two bricks wide. Then she hopped down and rushed over towards me, balancing the umbrella over my head.

A loud thunderous rumble in the sky sent kids and their grown-ups scattering as fast as they could. Nai Nai pulled me close, forcing me to link arms with her. The height difference made it awkward for us to walk side by side.

'Look at you, little nana's boy!' shouted Jay Jay as he ran past us to get into his dad's fancy car. I dropped my head down and hunched my shoulders.

Mitchell skipped by and flipped up the side of the umbrella so that Nai Nai let go and it tumbled out of her hands.

'Ah ya!' she exclaimed, tottering to retrieve it. Perfect. Another Nai Nai display for my schoolmates to laugh about. Nai Nai gingerly picked up the umbrella and began to pull its spokes back into some kind of octagonal shape. She started to chatter incessantly in her dialect. Her words were harsh – I could tell from the way she was saying them. We rushed along the pavement towards home, trying to keep dry, but the wind was blowing the rain at a slant. I didn't want her to shield me with her stupid wonky umbrella. I just wanted her to leave me alone.

My feet were soaking by the time we got back to the takeaway. I threw my sodden school shoes at the base of the stairs and pounded up in wet socks. Ma came into my room holding a laundry basket.

'What's wrong, Danny?' she said as she gently closed the door.

'It's Nai Nai – she came to school TWICE today!' I said, peeling my soaked-through socks from my feet.

'She wanted to bring you the umbrella, as you didn't take your coat. She thought it was monsoon weather. What's wrong? Why are you so wet?'

'I didn't want her to come. She should have stayed here.'

'Danny, that's unfair. I think you are being ungrateful.'

'It was embarrassing, Ma! First she comes with chicken feet and then she comes back to walk me home. Everyone was laughing at me!'

'No need to shout . . . shhh . . . She is coming up.' I heard small steps padding up the stairs. The door to my bedroom opened. Nai Nai was rubbing herself with an orange hand towel.

'She was doing a nice thing. She saw you didn't have breakfast and that you weren't wearing a coat. She was being thoughtful, Danny, unlike you,' Ma declared.

I wanted to get my clothes off. My school shirt was clinging to my chest. I got up and opened my wardrobe. A stack of Nai Nai's clothes tumbled down from the top shelf.

'Arghhh! And this stuff in here. It's my room! I WISH SHE WASN'T HERE! I WISH SHE HAD NEVER COME!'

I turned around, about to go to the bathroom to get changed. Ba was standing in the doorway, a pained expression spread over his face.

8

A Pain in the Back

'Danny Chung! I – I –' Ba spurted out. His face was red and contorted. He tried to stand more upright but then leaned against the wall. Silences from Ba were worse than when he told me off. He was too upset even to do the Chinese Way lecture.

He gathered himself a little more.

'Nai Nai just wanted to be there for you, that's all. She didn't get to see you for the first eleven years of your life and so she wants to see as much of you as possible.' Ba winced and put a hand on his back.

Ma turned to Ba and stroked his upper arm

with her free hand. 'Danny and Nai Nai just need time together. That will fix it. Are you all right?' She put down the laundry basket.

'It's just my back . . . it's been a little painful for a couple of days.' Ba had never hurt himself like that before. 'I think it was making that bunk bed,' he said, nodding towards the towering white bed in my room.

'Here's what we're going to do. I'll carry on doing the laundry,' said Ma, picking up the clothes from my floor. 'You, Danny, will help more and spend time with Nai Nai. And you . . .' she said, looking at Ba. 'You will go rest.'

'It's nothing. Here, I'll carry that washing for you. See, there is nothing wronnngggg!' He took the basket from my mum's hands but then dropped it. All of my dirty clothes fell out. 'Argghhhh!' Ba was slightly bent over to the right. One hand was holding his back. The other grabbed hold of the door frame to my room.

'What's happened to you?' Ma asked. Her face looked concerned. 'You can't stand up properly.' She gathered the clothes and put them back into the basket.

'She's right, Ba. Do you need to go to the

hospital?' I was worried that my ungratefulness had caused Ba to go into spasm or something. However, I was also relieved that he was distracted from what a terrible grandson I had been.

'I'm not going anywhere. I'm not finished with you.' He turned to go back downstairs, but one of his legs buckled.

'Ouch,' I said.

'Arghhh!' he screamed. He held his side much tighter this time. He couldn't conceal how much pain he was in any longer.

'That's it. You go lie in bed. I'll sort it out,' Ma said, ushering Ba into their bedroom. I heard the relief that came from lying down. Ma reappeared a few moments later.

'I will do the cooking instead of your ba, and Nai Nai can help you take the orders; it will only be for a very short time. It's always quiet early in the week,' Ma said, holding my shoulder. I felt my stomach lurch. I wasn't very good at this kind of thing. Obviously, I'd seen Ma serving the customers thousands of times, yet I had never done it myself. And how was Nai Nai going to help, when she didn't speak any English? I felt

my legs buckle just like Ba's. What if I got the sums wrong? What if I gave people the wrong change? My head was full of maths symbols clanging into each other.

Nai Nai had mysteriously changed into a tracksuit and slippers. Ma explained what had happened to Ba, and Nai Nai produced a tiny pot of Tiger Balm and headed into my parents' room. Ma left after.

'But, Ma, I don't think I –' I followed her to my parents' bedroom where Ba was groaning as Nai Nai turned him over and started rubbing the menthol-smelling goo onto his back. Ma was pulling off his slippers in a very rough manner.

'You can do it, Danny. It's just finding the number on the menu, writing it down and adding up the total.' Adding up? I can add, but I don't know about doing it under pressure.

'Arghhhh! I'll be all right in a minute!' shouted Ba as Nai Nai touched a part of his back that was really sore. He tried to sit upright, but she pushed him back down. She was doing some kind of massage on him now.

'Ma, I kinda have this maths thing I need to start . . . I was hoping to go over to Ravi's place to work on it . . .' I knew she wasn't listening to me. Ba's groans were drowning out my already quiet voice.

'You lie down or you'll never get better!' Ma said sternly, pointing to Ba. Then she turned to me. 'We can handle it, right, Danny? The Chungs have got this! Team Chung! I don't want to waste the food we've already prepared. But maybe I can get Adrian to help out later.' She grabbed her phone. I knew she was texting Auntie Yee to find out. Uncle Yee had been in the catering business for a long time and was semi-retired.

I reluctantly nodded my head. The maths brainstorming session with Ravi would have to wait. Instead, I would have to hang out with Nai Nai . . . again. Ma walked out, leaving me and Nai Nai to nurse Ba.

Ba turned his face towards me. 'Your Nai Nai, she's very quick with numbers. Her mind sees the numbers like a human calculator. She can . . . arghhh . . . help . . . Danny . . . with the money.

Lucky dragons, I told you.'

Nai Nai was warbling as she rubbed his side – this was a Tiger Balm moment. I think she was enjoying looking after Ba as well.

'She was a high-school maths champion,' Ba continued. 'And when I was growing up she used to love finding out about all different kinds of maths, not just adding up . . . arghhh . . . Ma! She was the practical one in our family . . .' My dad looked funny. Like he was remembering something.

Nai Nai laughed and carried on rubbing in the ointment. He said something to her and she nodded. 'Hao hao,' Nai Nai said.

'Danny, I know it's not easy having her here . . . but she is so happy to see you. Can you please make a little effort? Please? Just for me?'

I felt bad for saying horrible things about not wanting her here. Ba was happy to see his mum and now he was in pain. I guess I could try.

Ma peered around the bedroom door.

'Okay,' said Ma, 'Clarissa says that Adrian can come and help out tonight, and maybe tomorrow, but not until after eight. So I will still need you and Nai Nai to man the counter for a few hours. It's good she's here, otherwise we'd be really stuck.'

Nai Nai hopped off the bed and held her hands up. The menthol smell filled the room.

I went to the living room to ring Ravi and let him know I couldn't come over. I was working with Nai Nai.

9

Ant Gran Makes a Friend

I stood up tall, waiting for the first customer to come in. The pen in my hand nervously tapped the white order pad. It had the order number in red at the bottom, to be ripped off and given to the customer so that when it was called from the kitchen they knew their food was ready. My stomach felt like it was doing somersaults. Nai Nai was firmly planted at the table by the TV with a mound of fruit in front of her.

'You don't need to wait like a meerkat for the customers, Danny,' said Ma. 'Sit down, watch the TV. When they come in, then you can stand up.

Nai Nai is here to keep you company. Remember to smile.'

'All right, Ma, I'll try my best.'

I looked over at the table. Nai Nai was sucking on a half-eaten plum; the juice was running down her chin. She wiped it with a serviette. She was watching someone dancing on the telly and was obviously enjoying it. It was a show where men dressed up as women – very glamorous women.

The front door opened and an older lady came in. I'd seen her in here before, but I'd never talked to her. I hoped she was going to be nice.

'Ohh, I love that show. Gorgeous men dressed as gorgeous women. We never saw much of that when I was a wee lass.'

'My mother-in-law has never seen anything like that before, she can't believe it,' said Ma, standing by the kitchen door. 'Hi, Mrs Cruikshanks!'

'Hello, Sue,' the customer said, the whiskers on her chin bobbing up and down as she chuckled.

'This is my son, Danny. He'll take your order. I've got to cook tonight.'

'Oh, I hope nothing's wrong with your other half.'

'He's upstairs. Bad back. He'll be okay

in a couple of days. Danny, take care of Mrs Cruikshanks. She is a regular.' Ma quickly turned and disappeared. It smelt as if something might be burning.

'Okay, young man?' said Mrs Cruikshanks. She was wearing a long beige coat. The cuffs were dirty around the edges. She rested her arms on the counter.

'Yes. I'm fine.' I didn't feel fine though; my hands were shaking.

'So, I usually have the same thing every week. Chips and chicken chowmein. Sweet-and-sour pork if it's my birthday!'

'Okay.'

'Is that yer wee nanny, then?'

'Yes, she's my nai nai. She arrived a couple of days ago.'

'Hello, love!' Mrs Cruikshanks started waving at Nai Nai.

Nai Nai got up and wiped her hands on a tea towel hanging over the back of her chair. She approached the counter and stood on two trays of Coke cans so she was the same height as Mrs Cruikshanks.

'Hell-oh,' Nai Nai said. It was a pretty good

attempt at a hello. Nai Nai seemed happy someone was taking an interest in her.

'You been enjoying living here? It's been wetter than a week in Glasgow. Global warming, I think, although there are some down at bingo who swear it's all a conspiracy,' said Mrs Cruikshanks. 'Ohh, what's that you're drawing?' I had doodled on the order pad without thinking about it.

'Oh, that? It's a cat on stilts,' I replied. 'Do you like playing bingo?'

'Your drawing is fab. Yes, I love bingo. I go almost every day. Last week, I won a bottle of eau de parfum by a girl group called Little Minx or something. It stank to high heaven, so I gave it to the charity shop. But you can win some great stuff – vouchers, chocolate . . . which is how I lost all my teeth.' I looked at her smile. She seemed to have a full mouth of perfect white teeth. I was confused.

'I've not seen a bingo hall around here. Where do you play?' I asked.

'It's at the Longdale Community Centre, around the corner from the park. They have bingo every day at 2 p.m. Then one Saturday a month it's the Grand Bingo Prize. I've never won it myself, mind, but we can only hope. Your gran should try it. There's over-sixties yoga too, but there's no way I'mma doing that, I'd end up in hospital . . .' I imagined her trying to get her legs around her head – it was a funny image. I would have to try to draw that later.

'Do you know what food you want to order?' I asked, feeling very grown up, pen at the ready.

'Yes. No . . . hang on.' She was still scanning the menu on the counter. Her fingernails were long and slightly yellow as they went down each column on the menu.

'Shall I be adventurous? No . . . I'll have my usual today, chips and chicken chow mein. Numbers 92 and 67.'

I wrote down the numbers and the price of each item.

'Wait! I'll have some prawn crackers and a can of Coke too,' she added. I wrote down the amounts on the notepad.

I could feel Nai Nai right beside me smiling at

Mrs Cruikshanks and glancing at the order pad. It made me nervous and I couldn't think straight. I scanned under the counter to see if I could find the calculator. Our till was a relic. It didn't add up when you pushed the numbers and only one button worked that opened the cash drawer.

'Ma! I can't find the calculator!' I shouted as I rummaged around.

'I'm too busy frying, just add it up on the order pad!' Ma shouted back. I felt my palms getting sweaty.

'How much do I owe you, young man?' Mrs Cruikshanks asked, tapping her fingers on the counter.

'Sorry . . . hang on.' I bit the side of my mouth. My brain was turning to mush. I started twisting the pen lid. My neck was beginning to feel hot.

Nai Nai leaned over gently and I slid the pad towards her, giving her a hopeful look. Ba said she was a maths champion, after all. She took the pen from me and in a few seconds she'd written down the total sum. It was like *zap zap zap* and she knew the answer. She didn't even write down the bits you carry over. She was fast! She slid the pad back to me. I breathed a sigh of relief.

'That's twelve pounds twenty-five, please.'

'Here you go, young man.' Mrs Cruikshanks gave me the money and Nai Nai opened the till and without hesitation gave Mrs Cruikshanks her change.

Ripping off the order slip, I took it into the kitchen to Ma. I eyed the sharp spike where she would impale the slip once the order had been cooked. I kept my distance; the kitchen was full of loads of things that looked like they could cause major damage.

'Are you doing okay out there?' asked Ma, turning to look at me quickly. The flame on the hob was huge as she poured some oil and swirled it around the wok a few times. The clanking noise of the wok hitting the gas ring was loud. She switched on the overhead industrial fan.

'Yes. Nai Nai is quick at maths, isn't she?' I shouted.

Ma yelled, trying to be heard over the fan, 'You're doing great, Danny! She smiled at me as she threw some chopped onions into the wok, then dashed in some vegetables and pieces of chicken.

'Thanks.'

I went back to the counter area. Nai Nai

had opened the hatch and was sitting with Mrs Cruikshanks. She was offering her some lychees.

'Oh, what in name of *Corrie* are those slimy little things?'

'Lychees,' I said.

'Leeches?'

'No, lychees. They're from China. My mum says Nai Nai loves them because they remind her of home. They grow in her province.'

Nai Nai was talking away and Mrs Cruikshanks was smiling and nodding. They looked like old friends.

'Well, I've never tried anything like this eyeball-looking thing before. But I'll give it a go. Your granny is fabby. She's got such a kind face. I don't understand a word she's saying, mind, but I know a good 'un when I see one.'

Ma brought out the bag with the takeaway containers in it, put it on the counter and popped in a can of Coke from the pack Nai Nai had been standing on.

'Here you go. Enjoy!' Ma wiped a bead of sweat from her brow and then disappeared back into the kitchen. Nai Nai got up and waddled to the counter area. She picked up an orange and put it into Mrs Cruikshanks's takeaway bag.

'Thanks, love. Hey, you should come to bingo. I'm there every afternoon.'

Nai Nai didn't know what had been said, so I stepped in.

'Yeah, that sounds like a good idea. I'll tell her about it.'

'Good lad, see you, love!' She picked up her food and left.

Phew! We did it! Nai Nai and I had served our first customer and it wasn't that terrible. Mrs Cruikshanks had been really friendly. I didn't know why I had been so worried.

Next, a couple of young people came in – a man and a woman – older than Ravi's sisters, but not 'old' like my parents.

'Hello, how can we help you?' I said, smiling at them like Ma had told me to. Nai Nai was standing next to me, ready with the pad and pen. I was actually grateful that Nai Nai was there to help with the adding-up bit.

'We'll have two prawn in black-bean sauce, one egg-fried rice, one boiled. Crab and sweetcorn soup and a portion of apple fritters,' the woman said really fast.

I pointed to all of the items the lady had mentioned. Nai Nai jotted them down in quick time and in a flash had added up the total.

'Fifteen pounds and eighty-nine pence, please,' I said, looking over at the pad.

'Do you take card?' the lady asked. The man went to sit down and was using his phone.

'We do contactless – just touch it here,' I said, holding up the card reader. 'Thanks, it'll be about ten minutes.' I took the order into the kitchen. When I came back two more people had arrived. Nai Nai was smiling at them and nodding. The woman she was serving was pointing at the numbers and she was writing down the amounts.

Two and a half hours flew by. We'd had a rush of people ordering, but it had eased off, leaving the takeaway quiet for a while. Ma came out from the kitchen and slumped into the chair. I could tell her feet were aching from standing up all the time. I didn't know how Ba did it every day.

'You two have been great. I'm shattered from cooking in there. It's so hot.' She poured herself a mug of cooled boiled water from the flask and picked up an apple to eat.

Nai Nai and I sat down too, but I kept looking at the door, ready to spring up if a customer came in.

Nai Nai said something to Ma, then picked up a peach and bit into it.

'Shuxue,' Nai Nai said to me. Ma smiled.

'Ma, what's *shoe share*?' I asked. 'Nai Nai has said it a few times tonight.'

'Oh, shuxue means maths. She can help you with your sums if you like, and maybe one day you can do the adding-up yourself. Although, we have a perfectly good calculator somewhere. I wonder if your ba left it in his car. We should get the till fixed, but all these things cost money.'

'And how come she understands our numbers? Don't Chinese people use symbols?' I knew that one, two and three were just vertical lines in Chinese.

'They understand numerals too. It's a universal language,' she said. 'I'd better get back to the kitchen. I hope your ba's back heals soon; I don't want you working here too much.'

The door opened wide and instead of a customer it was Auntie and Uncle Yee.

'Panic over! We are here!' Auntie Yee had

on flat shoes and black trousers, and her hair was tied back. She was holding onto a designer shoulder bag and in her other hand she had a pair of yellow rubber gloves. Ma smiled as Auntie Yee slid them on.

'Adrian, you cook. I can keep Su Lin company on the counter. We have come to save the day. Yet again.' Uncle Yee shook his head slightly. He came up to me and gave me a fist bump.

'Hi, little man. I heard your dad hurt his back?'

'Yeah, he's upstairs in bed.'

'I'll go and check on him,' said Uncle Yee. He took off his trainers and bounded upstairs. I was relieved he was here.

'Amelia is at home working on her maths project. We've got the webcam on so we can see her,' said Auntie Yee, tapping her mobile phone. I was thankful I didn't have to put up with Amelia today, or being spied on by my parents.

'This must be your Nai Nai.' Auntie Yee said something to Nai Nai, and Nai Nai nodded and then said a few words back.

Uncle Yee appeared from the stairs carrying some empty mugs. He put on Ba's red apron, which was hanging over the chair, and tied it tight.

'Right, I'm ready to get cooking! Good job, Danny, for helping your mum. You and your Nai Nai can go rest now. We've got your back.' He gave me a high-five.

Auntie Yee took off her shoes and the rubber gloves and sat down. 'Adrian, before you begin, make me a ginger and lemon tea?' she said to Uncle Yee.

'Certainly, Your Majesty,' he said, mock-bowing to her.

'Thanks, Danny. You and Nai Nai helped a lot. Go to bed now – school in the morning,' Ma said.

Ma led Uncle Yee into the kitchen and I heard the kettle being put on.

Nai Nai and I were happy to head upstairs, out of the way of Auntie Yee, who had already turned off the TV. It was just past nine and I was so tired, having not slept well for the past few days. I would work on my maths project another time. I hoped Ba's back would get better soon.

10

Blank Brain Syndrome

Thank Fat Buddha, it was Friday. Finally! I had been struggling all week to keep awake at school. Nai Nai and I had helped on the counter nearly every evening until Uncle Yee could come to take over from Ma in the kitchen. Ba had slowly been improving and could at least hobble about now. Last night he did a short stint behind the counter and was happy to be on his feet again.

Before I left for school, I quickly sketched a rhino

who had candles instead of horns. He was going around lighting stuff, making wishes and running away from other animals who were trying to blow out his candles. I was having so much fun with it that I forgot the time and had to run to school. The bell had already rung by the time I got to the playground. I'd missed lining up.

I ran to my class and saw Ravi sitting in my chair next to Tia. They were laughing about something. Ravi saw me and did a little wave, then went to his seat. Tia turned around and said something to Mitchell, who then got out his phone and started typing.

'You look tired,' said Tia, with a funny look on her face. 'Anything or anyone keeping you awake at night?'

'Yeah, I'm totally wiped out.' Something felt off. Tia asking me a question was weird. I turned behind me to speak to Ravi. He looked a bit pale, as though he was coming down with a cold.

'Hey, Sir Ravi, did you come up with any ideas for the maths project?'

'Yeah, I think so. I'm doing hip-hop fractions. My cousin Deep is going to help me with the turntables. Do you need help?'

'Yours sounds cool. I need a miracle. Are you free to meet up in the Easter holidays to help me out?'

'I am free Tuesday, I think,' said Ravi. 'Monday my aunts and uncles are coming over for lunch – shhhh. Quick, turn around, Mr Heathfield is here.'

I swivelled around just in time.

Giggles and whispers began to erupt all over the classroom.

'Settle down, please,' said Mr Heathfield.

I did a massive yawn. I couldn't help it.

'Late night, Mr Chung? Or am I boring you?'

'Yes, sir – I mean, no. Not boring, sir.'

Mitchell put his hand up.

'Yes, Mitchell?'

'Danny's tired because he shares a bunk bed with his nana!' Mitchell blurted out.

'And she farts in the night, sir!' added Jay Jay. The whole class erupted with laughter. My face burned red hot. I slunk further down into my seat. I wanted the earth to open and gobble me whole. It made sense now. Tia asking me why I looked tired. Mitchell texting – that's what they were all laughing about earlier. How could they know? Who'd told them?

'Quiet! The sleeping arrangements of your classmates are no concern of yours,' said Mr Heathfield. He came over to me and spoke gently. 'Mr Chung, pop to the office. I've forgotten the register. You can pick someone to go with you.' I pointed to Ravi, who slowly got up out of his seat.

I bolted out of my chair, not looking back. I felt Ravi looming behind me. Mr Heathfield was doing me a favour – I needed to be out of there. Everyone knew about Nai Nai sharing my bedroom. It was the worst of the worst. I would never live it down.

'Hey, Danny, wait up,' said Ravi, poking me in the side.

'Not now, Ravi,' I huffed, my fists bunched tight.

'You all right?'

'Do I look all right?' I said. 'It's literally the worst day at school ever. I can't think of a maths project, my brain is a blank right now, AND I'm trending as the fool of the whole class, and I'm just so tired.'

'I'm sorry,' said Ravi. He picked up the register from the office table and we walked along the corridor.

'I just don't get it,' I wondered aloud. 'How do they know about the bunk beds? The bus stops outside our takeaway and some people can see into my bedroom. Do you think that was it?'

'Maybe,' said Ravi. 'Do any new drawings this week?'

'Just one, I'll show you later. I've hardly had any time – what with all of the counter work I've been doing with Nai Nai. But my dad's back is nearly better now. He's going to work tonight. I'm so glad it's the Easter holidays as school sucks right now. Hopefully by the time we come back everyone will have forgotten all about Nai Nai and be onto the next thing they find funny.'

'Yeah, I'm looking forward to it too.'

I kept my head down for the rest of the day. I couldn't wait to get out of there.

As I left the school gate, I heard someone behind me. Ravi was coming towards me. 'Danny, wait a minute, I have to tell you –'

But then suddenly Carter was by my side. 'Hey, Danny.' Was he going to rub it in more?

'Don't worry . . . it's nothing.' Ravi waved and ran off down the road to his mum's car.

'Hi,' I said to Carter nervously.

'Erm . . . that rubbery cake thing you gave me to shoot at the other day – it was well funny trying to hit it. I was wondering if you wanted to hang out at the park next week? I have a spare blaster gun if you have any more of those cake discs we can shoot at? I'll tell the boys to behave, okay? I know they can be a bit . . .'

'Oh, yeah, don't worry about it . . . that would be great. What day?' I didn't want to seem too eager, but I was bursting inside! Ravi and I had NEVER been invited to play with Carter and his gang, and the best thing was that I'd get a chance to play with the blaster guns.

'How about Tuesday at two?'

'Definitely. It's on.'

'Cool. See you near the bandstand at two then. Oh, and come alone. I only have one extra gun.' I knew what he meant: don't bring Ravi. 'And . . . well . . . I thought you should know. It was Ravi who spilled the beans about you sharing a bunk bed with your nan?'

I felt my stomach lurch.

'I didn't know that.' How could my best friend do that?

'Yeah, well, maybe he's not who you think he is. See you on Tuesday, then.'

'Yeah, totally, I'll definitely be there . . . by myself. Thanks, Carter.' I was feeling all over the place. I was happy I was going to play blasters with Carter, but why had Ravi told everyone about my nai nai?

When I got home my parents and Nai Nai were sitting at the dining table, shelling prawns together.

Nai Nai held one up with its face still attached and wiggled it about. 'Dan Dan, hell-oh.' I almost grinned.

'How was your day? Are you all right?' Ba asked.

'I'm okay. Glad school's finished,' I replied.

'Danny, I'm back in the kitchen tonight,' Ba said. 'To thank you for helping out, we've decided you have no chores for the whole of next week, and as an extra treat we'll give you some spending money for snacks and entrance fees – you'll be able to do fun stuff with Nai Nai every day. You can take her to the park, find her some activities, and maybe she will make a friend?'

'But –' I began.

'No buts,' said Ma, 'otherwise she's just around the flat and me and your ba have to work as usual. She's so excited to spend quality time with you.' Ma and Ba, double team, back together again.

'Yes, she worked really hard too,' Ba added. So we want her to enjoy herself . . . with you. She's super excited.'

My heart dropped. I had to GRANNYSIT Nai Nai every day?

'But I'm busy. I've got things on with my friends and I have an important maths project due in straight after Easter. Can't one of you take her out?'

'No arguing, Danny, ' Ma said. 'You will look after Nai Nai and find her lots of nice activities to do. She said she is up for anything. And you get on so well now, after working together – you can bond even more. Anyway, it's not the whole of the Easter holidays. You, Nai Nai and I are having dim sum with Clarissa and Amelia on Monday, at lunchtime. That will be fun,' she added.

I took a deep breath in, looked at Nai Nai – who was now talking to a naked prawn – and sighed. Why me?

11

Dim Sum Love!

After forty-five minutes wedged between Nai Nai and Amelia in Auntie Yee's car, we finally arrived at Chung Ying in Birmingham's Chinatown. I often think that the only reason my mum hangs out with Auntie Yee is because she sometimes drives her places as Ma can't drive and Ba is always using the van for trips to the wholesalers. Ba and Uncle Yee had declined the customary school-holiday dim sum meet-up. Ma had been looking forward to taking Nai Nai out for a lovely meal. We walked from the car park to the entrance. The automatic doors zoomed open and my head was filled with Cantopop and the smell of wonderful fried and steamed food.

Nai Nai rushed to the fish tank and indicated for me and Amelia to join her. I went over, but Amelia followed our mums and the waiter to the big round table. Nai Nai tapped the glass, trying to wake up a fish who seemed to be sleeping. A sign on the front said, 'PLEASE WATCH YOUR CHILD: DO NOT TAP THE GLASS'. A big-eyed black fish came to the side window. Nai Nai put her face right up to the glass and started making a fish mouth. It was really funny.

'Danny! Over here,' Ma said. Amelia and Auntie Yee were watching as Nai Nai and I made our way over to the table.

The place was filled with other Chinese people, which pleased Nai Nai; she looked around and grinned. Ma always said, 'You know a Chinese restaurant is good if there are lots of Chinese people eating in there.' I wondered if Nai Nai could somehow make some friends here, but it didn't look like the sort of place where you could just go up to someone and ask them to be your friend.

In the middle of the table was a glass disc the size of a manhole. I spun it around.

'Not now, Danny,' Ma whispered when she saw Auntie Yee glaring at me.

Nai Nai pointed at the wall. It had a massive scroll painting featuring a phoenix and a curving dragon with huge claws. I wished I had my sketch book and pencils here. I made a mental note to draw a phoenix-type creature in my next comic. Nai Nai passed me a biro and a paper napkin. I smiled, then drew a phoenix with a robotic fish tail eating a bowl of rice.

'Ah, they are coming around to take our order,' Auntie Yee said. She spoke to the bored-looking waitress in Cantonese, never once asking Ma or Nai Nai what they wanted to eat.

A different waiter came over and placed a large black teapot in the middle of the table and five small teacups without handles, which he flipped upright. He poured tea into all of the cups without even asking if we wanted any. Nai Nai picked up her chopsticks and started washing them in her tea cup.

'Why's your grandmother doing that?' Amelia asked me.

'I dunno,' I replied.

'Because in some parts of China the water isn't always clean, so you wash your chopsticks in hot tea to kill germs. Sometimes when you eat out you would do that,' Ma said.

'Don't they have dishwashers?' asked Amelia.

Auntie Yee said, 'Where Danny's grandmother is from . . . it's, well, a little backward. They don't have modern appliances like washing machines and dishwashers. We're so lucky here in the West. So civilised.'

'It's a little different, Clarissa. I wouldn't say *backward*.' Ma looked annoyed. 'My mother-in-law has just arrived, so she's got to get used to things here.' Her face had gone red. I felt like I could burst too. I was sick of Auntie Yee's little digs at our family. She didn't do it so much when Ba was around. Nai Nai dried her chopsticks on the cloth napkin and placed them neatly in two lines, leaning on the ceramic pillow.

Puffing out my chest, I replied, 'You can never

be too careful.' And I dunked the ends of my chopsticks in my tea just like Nai Nai had done. Then Ma smiled at me and did the same.

Nai Nai grinned and nodded. 'Hao-a, hao-a.'

'Amelia, sit on your chair straight,' said Auntie Yee. 'Why don't you show Danny your new blog post on your tablet?

Amelia huffed, then took out a tablet with a furry pink leopard-print cover. She swiped and tapped. She held it up in front of my face and rolled her eyes. I could tell she'd rather play games on the tablet so she could ignore me.

'Danny is doing very well,' said Ma. 'Nai Nai got him a violin music book.'

'Oh? I thought he stopped going to lessons – isn't that what you told me?' said Auntie Yee, raising her eyebrows. I didn't want to embarrass Ma, so I made something up.

'I'm just having a break from the violin, weighing up my musical options. I'll get back to it one day,' I said. I had been happy that Nai Nai hadn't asked to see me play the violin since she had arrived.

'Oh, that sounds like an achievement. Amelia is on Grade 3 of the piano now. Amelia, show

Danny your piano video.' She'd already told us that a million times before. Auntie Yee began to click her fingers at her daughter. I'm glad my mum didn't click her fingers at me.

Amelia threw her head back and then started swiping and tapping some more. She flashed the tablet at me and then muttered under her breath: 'Anything else while we're at it?'

Perfect Amelia didn't like being her mother's minion after all? Last time I saw her she wanted to leave before my bed was finished – maybe it wasn't because she hated me after all. Maybe it was because her mum was saying how she would win the maths project. That's a big statement to make, considering hundreds of pupils in the city were entering the same competition.

I wondered if she was glued to technology because she was tired of hearing her mother's voice harping on about how good she was at everything. Imagine having to live up to that standard! I would have exploded by now. I was grateful for the parents I had, that's for sure. Amelia's finger started to slide about the screen. I noticed she had a drawing app. She held up the screen to show me.

It had the words:

OMG! THIS IS SOOOO BORING!

I nodded in agreement. The droning on about school in the school holidays was definitely boring. The food was yummy though. I loved dim sum more than any other type of meal.

'Have you been to Knights of Old before?' I asked Amelia now her guard was down. Perhaps for once I would get an answer rather than a grunt.

'No, never.'

'It'd be cool to win the tickets, although I haven't even started my project yet,' I said, looking for sympathy and maybe some tips.

Auntie Yee had heard me. 'Oh, Danny, I don't know if you should bother entering. Amelia's teacher said she has a very good chance of winning. So, we'll see.'

Amelia groaned and rested her head on the table. She was busy looking at her tablet on her lap.

'How is your Nai Nai settling in, Danny? You must be so close.' Auntie Yee was having a laugh – she knew we had to share that bunk bed.

'She is doing fine,' said Ma. 'Danny is very happy to spend a lot of time with his grandmother.

They are making up for the many years apart. They are inseparable – they love each other so much.' Ma nodded at me as though she was urging me to agree.

'Inseparable,' I said.

'How wonderful – the younger generation taking an interest in the older generation,' Auntie Yee exclaimed.

Not long after a waiter brought bamboo steamers stacked on top of one another to form a tower and placed them on the glass disc. Nai Nai lifted off one of the lids and the steam flittered away. The succulent dumplings glistened on their circular white paper.

'Chi-a, chi-a,' said Nai Nai, dropping a ha gao dumpling into my bowl. I stabbed it with my chopstick and stuffed it into my mouth. It was so good. She carried on filling my bowl with different morsels of food and then began to feed herself. Ma just picked at the food and hardly put anything in her bowl.

'Danny is going to spend the whole of the Easter holidays with his grandmother, taking her out and finding fun activities for her to do. Isn't that right, Danny?'

'Sounds mega fun,' said Amelia sarcastically.

'Well, at least I don't spend my weekends being taken to loads of boring extra-curricular activities,' I muttered so the grown-ups couldn't hear. Nai Nai was watching me though. Then she looked at Amelia, who was pouting.

'Danny, what plans have you got for Nai Nai this week?' Auntie Yee asked.

'Well . . . I thought she might like to try bingo. One of the customers mentioned it,' I said.

'Oh, no. Definitely not bingo,' said Auntie Yee. 'It is a crass game played by the lower echelons, Danny. You should take her to lawn bowls. Many ladies from the Women's Society go there – she can get light exercise and converse with the right kind of people.'

'That sounds good, Clarissa, thanks for the suggestion,' Ma said.

Auntie Yee turned to me. 'It will be good for you both. This Easter is the perfect time to bond with her. We look after our elders. It is the Chinese Way.'

Not her as well . . . I'd had enough of that from Ba. I dropped my eyes to my bowl and started eating more. Nai Nai had made sure I was fed well. When we had finished, Auntie Yee got the waiter's attention.

'Mai dan.' *Time to pay the bill.*

'Clarissa, let me get it this time,' Ma said as she lifted her handbag from the floor.

'No need, no need. I'll pay.' Auntie Yee had already got her large purse out of her bag and laid it on the table. She lifted out three crisp, new twenty-pound notes and placed them on the small round plate that the waiter had brought over with the bill on it. She didn't even glance at the total amount, just put the money on and handed it back to the waiter. I noticed Nai Nai looking at Ma, who was saying nothing. We got ready to leave and walked to the entrance.

Nai Nai whispered something to Ma. Ma's face became flushed. We stopped behind Auntie Yee and Amelia.

'Clarissa, we'll take a taxi home. My mother-in-law wants to see the city centre some more,' said Ma. We'd never, ever got a taxi home before.

'Oh . . . if you insist,' said Auntie Yee. She seemed upset that she wasn't the one making the decisions. 'I'll let you know when I'm coming round next.' And on that final note, Auntie Yee and Amelia got into their fancy red car. I could tell Auntie Yee's pout meant she wasn't happy. She kept looking straight ahead as she drove off.

Ma waved. I limply lifted one of my hands. Nai Nai was muttering under her breath.

'What is she saying?' I asked Ma.

'She says that Auntie Yee and Amelia are like sour apples – smooth on the outside, but bitter on the inside. I hope Auntie Yee didn't hear when she said it before – she'll never invite us out again.'

Sour apples. I liked it!

'Come on, let's get out of here,' Ma said, smiling at me. 'Let's go to the bakery!'

I wanted to give Nai Nai the biggest high-five in the land. She got it. She knew. Someone apart from me could finally see Auntie Yee for what she really was – horrible!

Nai Nai looked at me and gave me a wink.

12

NOT Bowled Over

Nai Nai stood at the dining table packing her bag with fruits of all sizes: a kiwi, a grapefruit and a bunch of grapes. Did she think she was going on an expedition or something?

'But do I have to look after her ALL day?' I asked as I played with a piece of toast. Ba put his hands on my shoulders. Nai Nai was humming a little tune.

'Please, Danny, for me?' Ba said. His back was almost better, but he needed to take more breaks in the daytime to rest. 'If she's out then she's not worrying about me and my back. She really wants to spend quality time with you.'

'I have a lot of stuff I need to do . . . a maths project for one, and other things.' Carter had asked me to meet up at the park at two. There was no way I was going to miss playing with blasters for the first time ever. But how was I going to get there if I was *grannysitting* ALL day EVERY day? The sun was shining too.

'Danny, we want her to enjoy her time here with us. Bowls seems like a good idea,' Ba said. 'She has her free bus pass now so can go anywhere local.' I bit my lip as I thought about it. What if people saw me with her? They would think I didn't have proper friends and only hung out with my gran.

The phone rang. I picked it up.

'Hello?'

'Hi, Danny, it's Ravi. I was wondering if you still wanted me to help you with your maths project. You could meet me at the library around three and we can go on the computers there.'

I looked over at Ba and Nai Nai, then turned away from them, shielding the receiver with my hands. My belly fluttered. I gulped as my throat suddenly felt dry. I knew Ravi had betrayed me, and I didn't want to see him. But should I come out and tell him that I knew and that I was upset with him, or should I make up an excuse? I decided on the latter.

'Hiya, erm . . . no. I can't today, I have to be with Nai Nai all day. My parents just told me.'

Ba smiled and gave me two thumbs up. I wondered if Ravi could tell I was lying.

'Oh, okay then. I'm sure I can help you come up with something in time for when we go back to school. Maybe another day then . . .'

He sounded small. I glanced at Ba, who was scrolling on his mobile. Nai Nai was piling oranges onto the altar. I felt awkward.

'Ravi, my dad said I have to get off the phone now . . . I've gotta go.'

And I hung up the phone before he had finished saying goodbye. I didn't need a friend in my life who had spread rumours about me. Even if those rumours were true. Ba was looking at me weirdly.

'You could have stayed on the phone longer, Danny. I didn't say a word.'

'It's all right, I want to get outside while it's still nice. You know, so Nai Nai can have a good day out,' I lied, again.

'Wonderful,' Ba said.

'Gong gong qi che – hao!' Nai Nai said, patting the jacket pocket where she had slid the bus pass. It sounded like *Gong gong teacher* to me.

'She's excited to go on the bus,' Ba said.

'Okay, we'd better go then,' I said to Nai Nai, a bit deflated. It would be the first time I wouldn't see Ravi over the holidays, but it was his fault, not mine.

'Look after her, Danny. She's the only mother I have,' Ba said, smiling.

Nai Nai and I got on the number sixty-three bus, which was a new experience for both of us. Nai Nai wanted to go upstairs and sit in the front seats, even though we only needed to go three stops. I prepared her for what we were doing as we sat on the top deck.

'I'm going to take you to lawn bowls today. It's full of old people, like you, throwing balls – well, not throwing them. I guess they roll them.' I held my hands in a sphere shape and then proceeded to swing my arm by the side of my body to show her what I was talking about. To reinforce my explanation, I took out a grapefruit from her bag and swung it, but there wasn't much room on the bus to do it properly. I got out my sketch book and drew a little diagram of what Nai Nai would have to do with the balls.

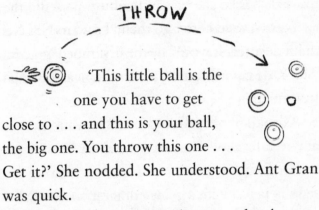

'This little ball is the one you have to get close to . . . and this is your ball, the big one. You throw this one . . . Get it?' She nodded. She understood. Ant Gran was quick.

'Okay,' she said. Wow, she was a fast learner, another new word to add to 'hello'.

'You will be fine. This is our stop!'

Nai Nai grinned. I pushed the red button and we made our way downstairs. Nai Nai pressed the red button too, multiple times. *Ding! Ding! Ding!* The bus driver gave us a *look* when we got off the bus.

The sun was shining bright and as we neared the bowling club I could see that the grass appeared flawless – two shades of green mowed in perfect straight lines. Nai Nai couldn't see over the hedges like I could. She would get to see the stripy lawn soon.

We stopped by the entrance and I turned towards her so she was in front of me. I did the swinging movement again, but this time added the sound effect *whoosh* and jumped up and down, doing a pretend victory dance. Nai Nai looked amused.

A group of old people dressed in white clothes and white shoes (and even white hats) were walking on the grass. Nai Nai was wearing her red silk jacket with a golden dragon on the back. I wondered if I should have checked the dress code before we'd come. Nai Nai stood out like a piece of char siu pork in a sea of white potatoes. One man paced up and down, then bent down at an angle, his eyes focusing on the grass. I wondered if he was inspecting the grass or whether it was some weird bowling ritual. A few of the ladies were chatting on the wooden deck.

As we rounded the corner I opened the green metal gate that lead us onto the path up to the clubhouse. Nai Nai stopped. She looked at all of the people. They stopped and gawked at us too.

'Hello there,' said a lady walking over the grass. 'Can we help you? Are you lost?'

'Hi, no, we're not lost. I'm Danny and this is my grandmother. We wanted to sign her up for bowls,' I said. A man stepped onto the grass and threw a white ball. It was shiny and a lot smaller than the ones with the red stripes on them that the lady was carrying.

'Oh, right, I see.'

'Come on, Marjorie!' shouted another lady. 'I'm waiting.' They were mega serious about this game.

'I'm sorry. If you go to see George in the clubhouse, he can tell you about the sign-up days for new players. Today we have a mini-tournament, I'm afraid. I really must go, but yes, see George.'

'That's great. It's just she's bored at home and it looks good for old –' the lady strolled away before I had finished my sentence '– people.'

'You don't have to be old to play bowls, young man. In fact, you can start at any age, even you could join our juniors,' said a man who had somehow crept up behind me. He was red-faced and had white hair that stuck up like fluffy clouds.

'I'm George. Come up to the clubhouse and I can give you the forms to fill in and the date for the next *newbies* meet, which is a fortnight away.'

I was disappointed that Nai Nai would have to wait, as we had already made the journey to get here and I'd be back at school by then. George led the way up the path to the white rectangular building beside the green.

I looked around at Nai Nai. She was transfixed by the game of bowls that had started on the lawn. At least she is interested, I thought. She smiled.

'Nai Nai, come on, this way.' I beckoned to her to follow, but instead she headed to the grass. Then she began to speed up, and her trot became a full-blown run. She put her hand into her bag and pulled out a bright yellow grapefruit. At first I thought she was going to offer it to the ladies as a thing of friendship, you know, like when you take oranges to a friend's house instead of chocolate because your mum says that's what Chinese people offer as a gift. It was like that, only . . . I could see her eyes. They were focused on the jack, the small white ball that the black ones had to get close to. I screwed up my face, not wanting to see but also not able to take my eyes away.

'Nai Nai!!!!' I began, but it was too late. I saw the sun-like bomb spin into the air, lobbed towards the green. The rest of the bowling ladies stood, mouths agape. The man whose game she had gatecrashed was running to try to intercept Nai Nai's makeshift ball. I held my breath, my arms outstretched.

'Please, no, not on the green!' George shouted behind me. He started to run too. I ran. Everybody was running!

'Who on earth is that woman?' someone asked.

We were all heading towards my four-foot grandmother and her grapefruit of destruction. ANT GRAN AND HER MIGHTY ORB would be the title of this particular comic scene.

I heard a gasp and then I saw it. Her grapefruit . . . spun and spun . . . its descent was imminent. It hit the grass and slowly bent around to the left. It kissed the white ball and to all intents and purposes Nai Nai was THE WINNER. I grinned even though we had to scarper quick.

'She's won . . . with a . . . grapefruit?' one of the ladies noticed, trotting over and staring at the yellow ball in bewilderment. She showed it to the group of bowlers, who were scratching their heads.

'Well, I never, a grapefruit. I wouldn't have spent that money on a new set of balls if I'd known you could win using a citrus!' laughed a man with a white comb-over hairdo. I was glad someone was finding it amusing. More onlookers came out of the clubhouse. The people near the lawn were pointing and some of them were glaring at us, a few tutting. We were disturbing the peace, it seemed. It was definitely a sign to leave as quickly as possible.

Rushing back to Nai Nai, I gently ushered her off the lawn, down the path and out of the gate. She turned and did a victory dance like the one I had shown her earlier. Someone kicked her grapefruit over. It rolled sadly towards us. I picked it up – it was a little battered and bruised but still looked edible, so I popped it into Nai

Nai's bag. She was looking around, wondering why we were leaving. I kept nodding and smiling through gritted teeth until we were safely back on the sixty-three bus, heading towards home. Lawn bowls had failed before it had even begun.

On the bus journey home, I couldn't look at Nai Nai. How was I supposed to explain that debacle to Ba and Ma? I was the one who had shown her how to throw a grapefruit.

Luckily Ma and Ba were out when we got home. I didn't want to have to explain why we were back so early; it wasn't even midday. Nai Nai went into the kitchen to make herself a pot of tea and came out ten minutes later with a plate full of guotie, or, as some people call them, potstickers. I loved them, but Ba never had time to make them for me any more. He was always too busy.

I grabbed some chopsticks and started munching them down after dipping them in soy sauce with a bit of cut ginger in it. Nai Nai's potstickers were SO good, just like Ba had always said.

I was not doing a very good job of keeping Nai Nai entertained. What activities could she do that meant I wouldn't have to spend my whole Easter holiday with her? Clouds of doubt were still whirling in my mind about whether I would be able to see Carter this afternoon.

Perhaps it was a miracle – who knows? – but the answer to my prayers passed the window. It was Mrs Cruikshanks. She had tied her beige trench coat around her waist and was walking along with large earphones on, bopping to music. I ran to the door and opened it.

'Hey, Mrs Cruikshanks!' I shouted, waving my hands wildly.

'Oh! Hello, young man. I'm listening to the Carpenters – before your time,' she said, turning around and walking back towards me.

'Did you say before that you go to bingo every afternoon?' I swung the door to and fro, excited that I might have a solution.

Mrs Cruikshanks leaned in like she had a secret. 'Yes, that's right, young Danny.'

'GREAT! What time does it start?' I asked. If my calculations were right, then I could drop Nai Nai off, run to the park to meet Carter and be back to pick her up in time for dinner. No one at home would have to know a thing.

'I'm on my way to the nurse at the GP – I've got bunions.' I didn't know what they were and I didn't want to ask. 'Bingo starts at two and I will be there. It would take a lorry to stop me from going. Why d'you ask?'

'Do you think Nai Nai would be able to play?'

'Of course. She's a quick wit, that one. Take her along and I'll see you there. I've got to rush.' With that, Mrs Cruikshanks carried on plodding down the road, her head bobbing.

A plan was forming in my mind. Bingo with Mrs Cruikshanks was the perfect and most obvious place for Nai Nai. She could stay there for a couple of hours AND it was close to the park. It was the perfect old-people crèche. Blaster time for me!

13

Lychees and Bingo Balls

Nai Nai and I arrived at the Longdale Community Centre and followed the arrow signs for 'BINGO', which were in big, bold letters. They led to a large hall where tables were laid out in rows and the lights were dim. On stage was a screen; it showed bingo balls bobbing up and down in a glass cube. Pink, green, blue, yellow and white balls jostling for space and attention.

I had enough money for twelve bingo cards, and I got Nai Nai a triple pack of marker pens that were red, because even I

knew that red was lucky in Chinese, and a token for a cup of tea or coffee and a custard cream at break time. These old people had it good. It was warm, they had snacks and they could basically sit in here all afternoon and play games. Sounded like a good life, if you asked me.

As I returned to the table where I'd left Nai Nai, I saw that a group of the old people had gathered around her. There seemed to be a commotion. I could hear people saying things like 'ashamed' and 'no way, Jose'. I hurried over with the cards and pens under my arms.

'Hello? Hi? Excuse me? What's going on? Where's my gran?' I squeezed through a wall of grey hair and knitted bags.

'Oh, you're with her, are you?' a voice said. It belonged to a very wrinkly lady who had bright blue candyfloss hair. She was tall and gawked at me as though I was a cockroach.

'Yes, I am. Nai Nai, are you okay?' I said, getting closer to her. I realised that even though Nai Nai was only little, she stood out like a sore thumb because she looked different. I knew how she felt.

'She has to move,' another voice chimed in.

This time it was a man. He was wearing a jumper the same as the blue-haired lady's. 'We always have these seats – without fail,' he asserted, and his leg began to twitch. As I peered through the crowd of bodies that had formed around us, I saw row upon row of empty seats.

'But there are loads of other spaces in here,' I said. 'Can't you sit somewhere else?'

'Cheeky little so and so!' said Mrs Blue Hair. I wanted to finger-joust all of them away from Nai Nai. She didn't seem so mighty with all of these people jabbering around her. In fact, she seemed small and a little lost. She was looking around at the scowling faces, wondering why they were angry at her. She put her apple core on the table, rummaged into her bag once more and pulled out a kiwi, offering it to the woman next to her.

'Look, she's new here, okay?' I said. When the woman shook her head, Nai Nai proceeded to get out a small teaspoon, cut the kiwi in half and start eating the inside with the spoon.

I heard a gasp and then a tut.

'You should call management, Enid!' the man in the jumper demanded.

Mrs Blue Hair ran off with her hand in the air,

trying to catch the attention of the lady who was standing by the exit near the side of the room. 'Linda! Linda, darling . . . over here!'

'Typical foreigners, coming here, taking our bingo seats . . .' said a woman who was all gums.

'Excuse me,' I said. 'I don't mean to be rude, and we didn't come to upset anyone, but are these seats reserved then?'

'Yes, that's where I always sit. Everyone knows that,' the man in the jumper said. He was beginning to go red.

Linda was coming over with Mrs Blue Hair, who was now pointing and moving her hands about. These people take bingo way too seriously.

'Hiya. I'm Linda, the manager here. Enid tells me that your gran is sitting in her spot. Formally there aren't any seats that are reserved, but the players generally like to sit in the same place. It's more a courtesy, really.' The manager was obviously trying to be diplomatic by not upsetting her regulars but also not causing offence to us.

'But all the chairs are the same,' I said. I was feeling angry. Nai Nai should be able to sit wherever she wanted. Even though she'd been driving me up the wall for days, I felt weirdly protective of her all of a sudden. I put the bingo cards down on the table and placed the markers carefully along the top so they didn't roll off. 'I'll speak to her – she doesn't understand everything I say, but I'll try.'

'They don't even speak the same language,' I heard someone mutter.

'Nai Nai . . . lai le? I think we could move over there by window. It's much better, hao?' Using my hands and fingers, I indicated eyes and screen.

She nodded. 'Hao hao.' Then she stood up. Everyone moved back and waited for her to gather up her bag of fruit. I picked up the pens and cards and we began to walk away from the rabble. I was relieved to see she was okay and not upset about the people ganging up on her. She was a tough old lady, my nai nai. As we moved away to look for a suitable place for her to sit, I saw someone waving frantically at the other side of the room next to the radiator.

'Cooooeeee! Over 'ere, love!' a voice piped up. The Scottish accent made it clear that Mrs Cruikshanks was here. Our saviour had arrived.

I'd never been so happy to hear the word

'cooeeee' in all of my life. Nai Nai recognised Mrs Cruikshanks and waddled over to her, beaming. I followed.

'Here, you sit by me. You don't want to be over there with that miserable bunch. I call them the Blighting Brigade, as they are blighters. They act like the hall is theirs and theirs alone. They're territorial at bingo, but you should see them when it's line dancing. It's like Hadrian's Wall. Impenetrable.'

Mrs Cruikshanks began to unpack a turquoise quilted bag with red tassels hanging from it. She took out a tall metal flask and a plastic plate like the ones you see toddlers eating from. Next to these she placed a plastic cup and saucer. She didn't stop there. She delved around in what seemed like the bottomless bag and pulled out a packet of five bingo markers and a cushion with cats on it that she plumped up before she plopped it on her chair. Then she got out a packet of chocolate macaroons and a photo of Jesus in a frame, which she arranged to her side. She finally sat down.

'Do you always bring so much . . . you know . . . stuff?' I asked.

'When you get to my age, Danny, you need to be comfortable wherever you go. Trust me, you'll be doing the same when you're an OAP.' I doubted very much that I would be carrying around a bag with tassels on it and my own cushion.

Nai Nai, not to be outdone, manoeuvred past me to just beyond where Mrs Cruikshanks had made herself at home and began unloading her handbag. Two kilos of lychees, one orange, another kiwi and a small flask containing just hot water – that is a Chinese thing. Even my parents never drink ice-cold water. They say it's bad for you. They'd be upset if they knew I loved filling my water bottle up at school from the water cooler in the lobby. Nai Nai sat down next to Mrs Cruikshanks and patted her friend on the arm.

I put the bingo cards and pens on the table. I looked around the room to see if anyone else had brought as much stuff with them as Mrs Cruikshanks and, to my surprise, most people had a stash of creature comforts. One man in a flat cap was already sucking on a sweet from a bagful that he had to his right. Another lady with two walking sticks had a sandwich and a packet of crisps to munch on.

Putting my hands in my pockets, I turned back to Nai Nai. She was copying everything Mrs Cruikshanks was doing. Mrs Cruikshanks straightened up her bingo cards and set her markers by the side. Nai Nai did the same gesture back. Mrs Cruikshanks put her two thumbs up towards Nai Nai and Nai Nai did the same gesture back.

I looked up at the big clock on the wall. It was nearly two. Carter said he would be at the park waiting for me. I had to go – now!

'Er, Mrs Cruikshanks, I have to leave now but I'll be back to collect Nai Nai when it's finished. When should I come back?

'An hour or so. She'll be as fine as a China in a bull shop!' She laughed. I didn't get it. 'You go, Tommy's ready now. It's eyes-down time.'

'Please don't tell my parents about this. Nai Nai's not supposed to be here and I'm not supposed to let her out of my sight.'

'No problem. What they don't know won't hurt 'em.'

14

Blast Off!

The park was busy. With school closed, loads of parents had brought their little kids. Carter was nowhere to be seen. I turned the corner by the bushes that look like choc ices. Then *pffff*, I felt something hit my back. Mitchell was there with two orange plastic blaster guns. He was wearing an ammo belt stuffed with foam pellets.

'You're late,' he said, smirking. 'That means you get a forfeit and I can hit you with as many pellets as I want for one minute.'

'Ahhh, that's not fair, is it? Where's Carter?' I was sure Carter had told me the others would be nicer. Shooting me in the back didn't seem like a good way to start.

'Life isn't fair. That's what my parents keep telling me.' Mitchell proceeded to hit me in the belly with five pellets.

He gave me a blaster half the size of his and a handful of pellets, which were threatening to fall on the floor. I shoved the pellets into the pocket of my hoodie.

'Is this the only one you have for me? It's a bit . . . small. Don't you have a larger one?'

'Nope . . . Mitchell called dibs on the other good one,' said Carter as he jogged over. 'My mum said we could all go back to mine after. Can you come?'

'No, I have to go get my . . . I mean I've got to pick something up afterwards.'

I aimed at the centre of the slide to practise my aim. Jay Jay ran over; he was wearing a khaki T-shirt like Mitchell. Both minions were here. Ergh.

'Are you ready for some aiming gaming? You're on my team, Danny,' Carter said, grinning. 'You didn't hit Danny already, did you, Mitchell?'

'No, no, we just had some friendly banter,

that's all.' Mitchell swivelled on his heels and ran off. His neon-green trainers were like beacons in the grass. 'But now it's on.'

For the first time in ages I felt free and was having fun running around and hiding. Carter was a pretty good shot. But that's probably because ALL he did was play computer games and shoot his blaster gun at weekends. It was good not worrying about Nai Nai following me, being alone or being stuck in the flat thinking about how bad I was at maths. I hit Jay Jay in the bum and that was five points. Carter was impressed and I was relieved. To be honest, I had never played before and wasn't sure I'd be any good, but our team was winning. We decided to give them a head start for round two. Mitchell and Jay Jay had an extra ten seconds to run and hide.

'Ready or not, we're coming!' shouted Carter.

That's when I saw him.

Sir Ravi of Longdale.

Oh no! I'd told him I was with Nai Nai all day. He was with his mum and little brother. Vishal was running over to the swings not far from where we were playing with the blasters. Ravi and his mum were talking. I ducked into a hedge and crouched down. I could hear my breathing; it was deep and fast.

My feet were beginning to hurt because I was on tiptoes. Carter gave me a wave. He pointed towards the playground where Mitchell and Jay Jay were hiding on top of the climbing frame. I knew that if I came out of the bushes Ravi would see me. Carter wasn't going to invite me again if I didn't move. Frozen to the spot, I shook my head. But Ravi was the one who should be apologising to me. This was a mess.

'What's the matter? They're sitting ducks,' Carter insisted.

I tried to think of an excuse. 'You go first. I'll wait and get anyone who runs off.'

Carter looked out. He clocked Ravi and his family, who were now near the playing area.

'Aren't you going to say hello to your "best friend"?' Carter said.

'Who do you mean?' I kept my head and gaze down, hoping that Carter would leave me alone.

'Danny's over here!' Carter yelled. He was standing up tall and pointing his blaster gun down at me. Mitchell and Jay Jay also saw our now-exposed hiding place. They began to run over to where we were.

'Shhhhh,' I hissed. I hunched my shoulders. I looked up and saw Ravi squinting in our direction. He pushed up his glasses. I stood up. For a second he looked surprised, then, when he saw me holding one of Carter's blasters, his face changed. He pulled up his hood and turned his back, shoving his hands into his pockets.

His mum said something to him, but he shook his head. I could tell he wanted to leave.

'Ahhh, he's not happy with someone,' Carter said, then laughed.

'He was the one who started it,' I said. 'Come on, let's carry on playing.' I glanced over at Ravi. He looked like he didn't know what to do with himself. He peered at me, then at Carter and Mitchell.

'I'm gonna get you!' Jay Jay shouted, coming towards me. I had to run for it or I'd get hit. I could see Mitchell. I ran, dived into the sand pit and pulled the trigger as I was falling. The pellet hit him on the back. He turned with a scowl on his face. My jacket was being pulled at. I looked down and Vishal was tugging on the corner of it.

'Hey, Vishal.'

'What are you doing? Can I play?'

'No, sorry. It's not my blaster.'

'Can I play if Ravi plays?'

I felt a stab in my chest. Ravi wouldn't want to play with me any more . . . probably.

Ravi was coming towards us.

'Vishal, get out of there. Come on, now!' His voice sounded strained. He wouldn't look at me.

'But Danny is here. Can we play too?' Vishal was trying to take the blaster out of my hands.

'No! Let's go. We don't want to play with someone who lies. Let's go.'

Mitchell was now running into the bushes. Carter was chasing Jay Jay round by the memorial benches with dead flowers tied to them.

'I'm not . . . Ravi, it's just that I wanted to . . .' How could I explain to someone I'd lied to that it was fun to play with Carter? It was different to playing with Ravi.

'You're busy with your grandmother, huh?'

'I was busy . . . earlier.'

Vishal ran off towards the swings.

'But now you are here . . . with them.' He lifted his chin towards the boys as they ducked and weaved through the bushes.

Ravi bit his lip and pushed up his glasses. He did that when he was nervous.

'Ravi! Can you push Vishal on the swing? I have a call!' Ravi's mum lifted her mobile to her ear.

'Bye, traitor,' Ravi said, turning and walking away from me.

'I'm the traitor? You're the one who showed me up at school. You're the traitor! You told everyone about Nai Nai sharing my bunk bed.'

Ravi looked at me. 'What I did was an accident. It just slipped out. I didn't mean to tell Tia. But you blatantly lied and said you were hanging out with your gran all day.'

My tongue felt tied. My mind went blank. I didn't know what to say. Ravi turned away and left. He walked over to the swings, lifted Vishal into one and gave a half-hearted push.

'Higher!'

Ravi pushed and Vishal swung into the sky.

His mum put her mobile into her bag and took over. Carter came and patted me on the back.

'Danny! Come on, they're running to the bandstand!' said Carter. Picking up my blaster with two hands, I jogged away from the playground and my former best friend.

'What time is it?' I asked.

'Dunno,' said Carter, and he shouted over the park: 'Jay Jay, what's the time on your phone?'

'Nearly three thirty!'

'Man, I've gotta go pick up my – go to the shop.'

'All right. Come out tomorrow if you want.'

'Thanks, I'll try to make it,' I said, handing him the blaster he'd lent me.

'Did you do your maths presentation yet?' Carter asked.

'Not yet. Haven't had time. What about you?'

'Yeah, I'm gonna do it on Fortnite . . . but it's not finished yet.' Fortnite? I should have known. If Carter wasn't on his blaster guns, he was playing Fortnite at home.

'Sounds . . . interesting,' I said. Even Carter had an idea. I was pretty much the only one in the whole class who had no idea what to do.

'I'll speak to you tomorrow about it. See ya,' Carter said. He, Mitchell and Jay Jay laughed their way towards the other side of the park where they lived.

It was what I'd wanted, to play with Carter, so why did I feel so sick inside?

15

Hao-si!

I was out of breath from running so fast back to the bingo hall to pick up Nai Nai. My chest hurt from the sharp intake of breath when I finally arrived. The doors were wide open and Nai Nai stood up from the bench in the lobby.

'Dan Dan-a!' she exclaimed. In her arms she had a bottle of perfume, a cuddly toy, a bag full of ladies' tights and a white envelope.

'Where have you been?' Mrs Cruikshanks asked. 'You've missed the show!'

'What?'

'Your nanny – she's something else! In all my years of coming here, I've never seen fingers so fast. Nothing like it, I tell you. She was banging spots on all of the cards like she was swatting midges at Loch Lomond. *Bam, bam, bam.*'

'What, she actually won all that stuff?'

'Won? She got Bingo four times and House once – when it mattered, mind you. She's got some little things and two hundred pounds' worth of vouchers for Freezer City. Imagine how much prawn cocktail you can get for two hundred quid!'

'Hao-si!' shouted Nai Nai.

'*Howse?*' I repeated.

'House . . . It's when you get all the numbers on the board. She got every single one. The Blighting Brigade were none too pleased, I can tell you. Enid was practically sulking. Her hair wasn't the only thing that was blue!'

'She should dye it green – with envy,' I said. I was so proud of Nai Nai. Her first time at bingo and she'd stormed it. I was always worrying that I would mess up – that's one of the reasons I didn't like maths, because I was scared I would get the wrong answer. Sometimes I didn't try things in the first place. But Nai Nai just had a go. She'd had a go at bowls and she'd had a go at bingo. Now look at her! She was so happy.

Nai Nai's eyes sparkled. She pushed the cuddly toy into Mrs Cruikshanks's hands – the furry gift was well received. Then she sprayed herself all over from head to toe with the perfume she had won – it was called Poison. What a silly name for a perfume! Mrs Cruikshanks coughed and then stepped back and put her hand to her mouth. I began coughing too.

'Jesus, Mary, mother of God! Not so much!'

'When are you going to bingo again, Mrs Cruikshanks?' I asked.

'When am I NOT going to be there, more like. I go every afternoon if I can. Some mornings I like to help out at the charity shop – Dogs for the Blind. Then Thursday mornings I'm at a tea dance. But the afternoons are for bingo. I can't get enough of it.'

'You do a lot of stuff.'

'When you get to my age you've got to keep busy. Mind you, next Tuesday I've got a woman coming to cut my toenails. Anyway, she's a star, your nan. Your folks must be proud – she's sharp as a tack.' Mrs Cruikshanks tapped her own head.

'Yes, both of them are very proud.' I imagined what they would really say if they found out that

I had left Nai Nai here with Mrs Cruikshanks, and secondly that she was playing bingo. 'They're both extremely happy that Nai Nai has a friend like you. So cultured and loyal.' You're going over the top again, Danny! Must be rubbing off from hearing Ma saying stuff like that to Auntie Yee.

'Oh, I have to tell you! You know what she did? I think it's her lucky charm. She was eating those round slimy things. Leeches.'

'Lychees.'

'Yes, that's what I said. She was pelting out the black bullets from her mouth and shooting them into a pile on the table. She offered me one but, to be honest, they give me the heebie-jeebies.'

Nai Nai was sniffing her Freezer City vouchers.

'No, no, Nai Nai . . .' I said, taking them from her hands. 'You can't spend those if you ruin them.'

'You'd better take her to Freezer City and show her what to do with them . . . GO GET YOURSELF A SEAFOOD PLATTER, LOVE!' Mrs Cruikshanks gave Nai Nai a gentle hug around the shoulders. And then Nai Nai turned and grabbed Mrs Cruikshanks and hugged her tight.

*

Taking Nai Nai to Freezer City was a revelation. She kept opening all of the deep freezes and sticking her head into them to see what was lurking inside. Her belly nudged against the side as her feet lifted off the floor. I imagined her falling forward and being trapped in a freezer forever. Ant Gran cryogenically frozen for eternity! That would solve my issues, and she would be permanently out of my room, but I was starting to feel a bit differently about her. She wasn't so bad after all. And now she was starting to make friends and get out of the flat, things would change. Maybe I wouldn't have to be the one to always chaperone her to places. Maybe Mrs Cruikshanks would be kind enough to take her around. Nai Nai might like to do some of the other activities that Mrs Cruikshanks did, like the tea dance. Dancing and tea sounded like something she would enjoy.

We arrived back home after six with five shopping bags full of frozen stuff, like chocolate-chip ice-cream (that is what I had picked), and Nai Nai had found a whole salmon that still had its eyes. She pointed to a dead fish eye and said 'Hao chi' – *how delicious*. Eyes. Fish eyes. Delicious? Gross. How were we even related?

Ma was wiping the counter when we got home. Nai Nai rushed forward to show her the bounty from the bingo hall.

'Wow, how did she get all of this stuff?' Ma took one of the bags and opened it. 'Fish and perfume?'

'Oh, she won it.' Nai Nai took the food into the kitchen where we had two large freezers.

'At bowls? They have prizes at the bowling club?'

'Er . . . yes . . .' Why didn't I just tell Ma the truth? 'They were having a raffle and she won. They pulled her ticket out of the raffle tin.'

'All of that stuff from one raffle ticket?'

'Uh-huh.'

'So you two had a nice day? You've been there a long time. I bet she was good at bowls, wasn't she?'

'Yeah, brilliant actually.' That wasn't a lie.

'And the people? They were nice?'

'Mostly . . .' I didn't want to tell Ma about being run off the bowls green, or the gang of oldies at bingo who made Nai Nai move seats.

Ba came through the front carrying a box of beansprouts. He put them on the counter, which annoyed Ma, then gave me a squeeze and ruffled my hair. 'Hey! How was your day?'

'He's been with Nai Nai all day – they only just got in. They're getting along so well,' Ma said.

'I told you, Danny. Having her here is really good for you. She can teach you lots of things about our history and culture. She won't be around forever. You're making your ba really happy. Well done, Danny. I'm really proud of you,' Ba said, disappearing with his box into the kitchen.

'You're welcome.' Surely the little white lies were fine. Nai Nai enjoyed her first bingo experience with Mrs Cruikshanks and I was out playing with my cool new friends. But I missed Ravi. I wished we weren't mad at each other. I felt bad that I'd lied to him now – even if he had let it slip about Nai Nai and me sharing bunk beds.

16

Skate Park Confessions

It was already the second week of the Easter holidays. I sat staring at my maths book, willing it to send me telepathic thoughts about what to do for my presentation. Ravi was doing a hip-hop fractions thing, Carter was doing something to do with Fortnite. Tia wouldn't tell me what she was doing. And Amelia definitely wasn't going to show me her project. Time was slipping through my fingers like sand and still my mind was a blank.

Ba's back was much better, but Ma still needed to help him with the food preparation and the trips to the wholesaler to buy the food supplies.

After lunch Ma handed me and Nai Nai a big chocolate egg each. They were wrapped in deep purple foil with puzzles on the back of the cardboard boxes. She said we could eat them straight away seeing as we didn't really celebrate Easter. I sat at the dining table unwrapping mine. Nai Nai pushed hers towards me and said something to Ma.

'She said it's too sweet. You can have hers too. She's happy with her fruit.'

I looked at Nai Nai. 'Thanks!' She tottered off upstairs.

'Are you taking her to bowls again today?'

'Yes, we're heading over there now.'

Earlier Nai Nai had nudged me when I was in my room tidying up and said 'Hao-si?' which I knew meant she wanted to go to bingo again because you have to shout HOUSE. I'd nodded but put my finger to my lips, hoping she wouldn't tell my parents.

'You're being so kind, Danny, spending your free time with Nai Nai. It's what we always wanted.'

I squirmed in my seat. Of course, I was actually going to drop her at bingo and then go meet up with Carter again. I stood up as Nai Nai appeared with her coat on and the woolly bobble hat that I hated.

'I've got one for Ravi too.' said Ma, holding up another chocolate egg. 'When will you be seeing him?' I looked around the table and saw she had actually bought a large cardboard box full of the eggs.

'Oh, I don't know. He's been really busy with family stuff, I think. I'll be sure to give it to him when I do see him though,' I said, not knowing when I was going to see my ex-best friend again.

Nai Nai came down and filled her bag with her favourite fruits and we left for bingo.

Mrs Cruikshanks greeted us and took Nai Nai into the bingo hall. I noticed a red Mercedes slowly drive by as I left the community centre and it reminded me of something, but I couldn't put my finger on it. I turned and headed to the park. I hoped Ravi wasn't going to be there again. Yesterday was pure squirminess. I had to put him to the back of my mind and try to have some fun. At least I didn't have to lie now or pretend I didn't want to hang out with Carter.

As I neared the concrete ramps, I noticed Carter had brought his black stunt scooter, and leaning against the metal fence was a slightly shorter blue one. His dad was just driving off.

'Hey, Carter,' I said, lifting up my hand. I noticed he wasn't wearing a helmet or knee pads.

'My brother said you could use his scooter. I wasn't sure if you had one.'

'Thanks. I do have one but it's from when I was little.' Ravi and I weren't really into these kinds of activities. I'd once had a go on Ravi's sister's skateboard and my bottom was not happy about it when I fell off. But if I wanted to keep playing with Carter, I would have to try to enjoy stuff like this a bit more. Scooting was much easier than skateboarding, so I thought I would be all right.

Carter showed me some of his moves. He was really good at spinning the scooter in mid-air. I hesitated when it was my go on the ramp. I stared down from the top and it looked like a long way to fall.

'Er . . . you can go again, Carter,' I said. 'I'll just scoot over there.' I pointed to the flat area next to us.

'Come on, Danny, don't think, just go.' Carter gave me a little nudge and I whooshed down the concrete ramp and whizzed back up the other side. My heart was racing. I'd done it without falling! And it was fun! I turned and grinned at Carter, who gave me a thumbs up.

We carried on scooting for a while and then sat and rested on the picnic benches. I'd brought some digestives in my backpack. I gave one to Carter, who scoffed it down in a couple of bites. Then I got out my sketch book. I looked over at Carter to see if he was going to ask me about it, but he was too busy eating the crumbs that had fallen into his lap. I shoved my biscuit into my mouth and grabbed my pens. I wanted to draw a snail on a skateboard going down a ramp before I forgot about it. I started to sketch.

'Do you wanna do the speech bubbles for this new comic I'm drawing? It's called **STUNT SNAIL**,' I asked Carter. I thought he might be into this one because he's good at scooting and doing stunts.

'Nah,' Carter said, peering over. 'Not my thing.'

'Oh, okay, right,' I said. I gazed at my sketch book. It was a really good character, but there was no one here to appreciate it apart from me. I shaded in the helmet that Stunt Snail was wearing, which had a star on it.

'Why's it got that fire coming out of its backside?' Carter asked.

'It's half rocket, half snail, and he's on a skateboard, and the fire is like rocket fuel.'

'Don't you think it's a bit . . . you know . . . ?'

'A bit what?' I asked. Awesome? Cool? Legendary?

'It's a bit . . . well . . . babyish? We're going to secondary school soon.'

'But I like drawing,' I told him, deflated.

'Put it away, the boys are here,' Carter said. Mitchell and Jay Jay were sauntering over the grass towards us.

I shut my sketch book and shoved it into my backpack.

'Have you asked him?' Mitchell said, raising his eyebrows and tilting his head towards me.

'Not yet . . .' Carter said.

'What is it?' I asked, feeling like I should leave the park and just head to the community centre to get Nai Nai.

'Well, seeing as us three have been kind enough to play with you –' Carter began.

'Yeah, we thought you could help us with our maths presentations,' Jay Jay said, wiping his nose on the back of his hand.

'My mum said all Chinese people are good at maths and that we should hang out with the Chinese boy in our year,' Mitchell said. 'I think you owe us, Chung.'

Stereotype city or what? I wanted to burst out laughing. Then the next second I wanted to cry.

'Well . . . sorry to pop your bubbles, guys, but I'm no good at maths.' I could sense things were turning sour. Very sour.

'Are you saying my mum is wrong?' Carter asked. 'But I let you use my stuff.'

'Carter, honestly, I'm not good at maths. I can't help you.' My fingers began to shake as I put my backpack straps on. It was definitely time to go.

'Can't or won't?' Carter asked.

'Really nice seeing you all . . . gotta go.'

'Okay, well, beware, Chung. Once you make an enemy of us, it's for life,' Carter said.

He pointed two fingers at me and then towards his own eyes, then back at me. I skulked away and then began to run towards the community centre.

17

Busted

Ma was folding sheets on the dining table behind the counter when Nai Nai and I got home from the bingo. Nai Nai took off her shoes and went upstairs.

Ma looked at me sternly. 'I know where you've been, Danny.'

Uh-oh, I thought.

'I specifically told you to take her to bowls. It's a gentle sport and she can get exercise. I did not tell you to take her to bingo.' I could hear echoes of Auntie Yee.

'But –'

'Let me finish. Clarissa called me. She saw you

leaving Nai Nai outside. She was all alone.' I knew
I recognised that red car.

'It's a community centre and she wasn't alone.
There's . . . a . . . community. Nothing bad
happened to her.'

'Clarissa said you weren't watching her; she
saw you in the park with a pack of boys.' A *pack
of boys?* She'd been spying on me.

'Do you always need to listen to what Auntie
Yee says?'

'You were supposed to look after her, not leave
her with strangers.'

'Mrs Cruikshanks isn't a stranger,' I pleaded.

'There is nothing more to say. You will go to
your room. You are grounded until you go back
to school.'

I wanted to scream, *I DON'T HAVE A ROOM
ANY MORE!* But I didn't.

I stomped upstairs to my – correction,
our – room. I tried to slam the door but Nai Nai's
dressing gown was hung over the edge of it so
it made no noise. I couldn't even bang the door
right. I flopped onto my duvet and stuffed my face
into my pillow.

Things couldn't get any worse. Could they?

Normally, Ravi'd be the one I'd call and we'd draw a comic about it and have a laugh. But things with us were in a right mess now.

Nai Nai's face appeared from over the side of the top bunk.

'Dan Dan okay?' she said.

'No, I'm not ok.'

She scrambled down the ladder and came to sit next to me on my bed. She put her arm around me and squeezed. I didn't mind it this time.

'It's complicated, Nai Nai. Ma said no more bingo. No more hao-si. Dan Dan – I mean me, I . . . am . . . in trouble. How can I explain it to you? How can I explain it ALL to you?'

I kinda wished I had picked up more Chinese language, because at times like this it would be good to tell someone how I felt. Right now I felt like a building was sitting on my shoulders. I'd seen Nai Nai with Mrs Cruikshanks – she had no idea what her friend was saying but she was listening all the same. That's like Ravi – he is a good listener. Not like Carter.

I got my sketch book from my backpack and started flicking through it. I came across the **ANT GRAN, SUPERVILLAIN** comic and quickly kept turning the pages, hoping Nai Nai hadn't seen that one. I flipped to the back page – the blank paper stared up at me. Nai Nai picked up my pencil case and rummaged through it. She pulled out a pencil and took my book. I almost grabbed it back off her in case she saw the drawings I had done of her. But I let her take it. She drew a heart with a smiley face. She was telling me she loved me.

I drew an angry ma, mouth open, baring her teeth and yelling. Then I drew some bingo balls and crossed them out like a 'no go' sign. An arrow indicated that the consequences for me were – a bed here, a few bars there, my sad face. She could see from my sketch that I was grounded in my room. I did a speech bubble with 'HELP!' in it.

'Then there's the maths project . . . shuxue, that's what you call it, isn't it? No good.' I pointed at my chest. 'I'm rubbish at maths, Nai Nai, and I don't know what to do.

Ba and Ma will be disappointed in me if I keep coming bottom of the class.' I drew some addition sums and other maths signs and then scribbled them all out. 'I bet you never had any trouble like this in China, did you?'

Lastly, I drew a picture of me and Ravi. Ravi was in one corner and I was in another. It would have been cheesy to draw a broken heart, but that's kinda how I felt. It had only been a few days, but I wanted him back. I wanted him to do my speech bubbles, to play finger-jousting, to come up with more excellent mutant dragon ideas. Being in the cool-kid gang wasn't all that fun anyway. But I guess you don't know until you try something.

'There's not much you can do about Ravi. I have to go say I'm sorry. Make it up to him. It's good to have a friend who understands you, isn't it?'

Nai Nai put her arm around me and gave me a side hug. I lay my head on her shoulder.

'Yes, we're friends, Nai Nai. I'm sorry to you too. You don't know what I've done.' I thought about the pictures I had drawn of Ant Gran being catapulted into the jaws of a dragon. I would get rid of them.

She rubbed my arm and held my head in her hands. When she smiled the whole of her face, wrinkles and all, lifted and it was like her whole face was one big smile. Then she got up and stretched her arms up high above her head, as though she was about to take off, like an **ANT GRAN SUPERHERO**. I felt much better just from showing her that I had a lot on my mind. It wasn't that I was just a bad grandson. I had been quite selfish. Ba and Ma were both right; we didn't know how long she would be here for because well, she was pretty old. I had to make the most of it.

She padded out of the room with her hands on her hips. Following her downstairs, I crept to the bottom step and stayed hidden. What was she doing? In the kitchen, I could hear loud voices. Nai Nai was practically shouting. She'd always been so calm since she had been here. Ma was saying something and Ba was trying to keep the peace. I heard my name but other than that I couldn't make out what was going on. Just then the kitchen door opened and Ma came out.

'Danny! Come down!'

I crept back upstairs to the halfway point and then started coming down, making heavy feet noises.

'Did you call me?' I asked, trying to look like I hadn't been eavesdropping.

'Yes, Nai Nai has spoken to us and she wants you to be ungrounded. She says it was her idea to go to bingo. Is that true?' She lied for me?

'Well . . .' I saw Nai Nai slink out of the kitchen. A hopeful smile lit up her face and her eyebrows were raised as if to say, *Tell them yes!* She urged me with her nodding head.

'Kinda . . . yeah, I suppose so. It's just at bowls . . . she had this grapefruit –'

'Ah . . . no need to explain further. You are ungrounded. BUT . . . you are not to take her there again, you understand me? I think Clarissa is right. It's not a good place for her.'

'Understood. No more bingo.'

I was ungrounded – thank you, Nai Nai. I looked at her and gave her the thumbs up when my mum's head was turned. I couldn't believe she had gone in there and given them what for. That was definitely the Chinese Way – elders always win.

18

No More Yees!

I flipped the sign on the front door to 'OPEN', then headed to the counter area. Business had been slow this week, probably because it was raining a lot. People liked to stay home if it was wet. I could hear Auntie Yee's heels clicking before I saw her. What was she doing here?

'Su Lin, I'm here!' she chirped while holding the door open for Amelia, who followed like a soggy rain cloud, her eyes rolling. She and her mother were in fuchsia today.

'She invited herself,' Ba whispered as he came through to the counter area with a large plate of expensive raw king prawns from the side storage area – he went into the kitchen without saying a word. He was probably annoyed that he had to cook extra food for them when they never invited us around for dinner. Auntie Yee sat down and took her coat off. I could hear Ba banging the wok around more than usual.

As usual, Amelia was told to hang out with me, so she reluctantly came upstairs into my bedroom. I was still cross at her and her mum for telling on me and Nai Nai for going to bingo. Uncle Yee was the only cool one in that family. The other two were the worst stirrers in history. We passed the living room door. Nai Nai was in there watching a show about baking cakes.

'How is it sharing your room with your nai nai?' Amelia asked as she moved my clothes from the chair to the floor. Then she sat down with her tablet in her hand, swiping right and then right again.

'You and your mum are snitches. Nai Nai was enjoying herself at bingo and you had to go and ruin it.'

'It was our duty to tell your mum we saw your Nai Nai there all alone. Goodness knows what could have happened to her. We were being good citizens.'

'I got grounded for two weeks because of you! Luckily I got out of it.'

'I just want to get out of here. I don't know why my mum bothers coming here at all.'

'She comes because she's bored and has nothing better to do than poke her nose in other people's lives!' The door to my room creaked open and Auntie Yee was stood there, her face as pink as her outfit.

'You despicable boy! How dare you be so rude?' she said.

Ma's head appeared round the door. 'Food is ready. What is going on here?'

'Your son has been saying things, about me – poking my nose in. I came here in good faith, Su Lin.'

'I'm sure we can all work this out. Danny doesn't mean it.' Ma was flustered; her face was going red.

'If this is how you raise the boy then he will not amount to anything, mark my words.'

Ma looked at me, disappointed yet again. I just couldn't seem to do the right thing.

'Danny, apologise right now,' Ma said.

'I won't say I'm sorry. It's Amelia this and

Amelia that. Auntie Yee only comes here to –'
I was cut off by Mrs High-and-Mighty herself.

'He's a troublemaker, Su Lin,' said Auntie
Yee. 'I told you that school was no good. You
should have gone private or at least sent him to
a good disciplined Catholic school. Look how
your child behaves and look at Amelia. There
is no comparison. You get what you pay for.'
Was she talking about me or the schools? I was
confused and angry.

'Amelia's mean and we all know where she
gets that from!' I shouted. 'You always take her
side, Ma!'

'Danny, you stop this right now.' Ma was
clearly embarrassed now.

'Amelia is definitely not a mean girl, she
is delightful,' Auntie Yee announced. 'Come
Amelia, we are leaving.'

And with that Auntie Yee grabbed Amelia's
arm. Her lips were pursed together. Her eyes
gleamed like daggers towards me. Then they
both disappeared downstairs.

'Wait! Wait, Clarissa!'

Ma's mouth hung open for a second or two,
then she turned to me. I could see that her brain

was trying to work out whether she should try to find a peaceful solution or admonish me. She chose the latter.

'Danny! I can't believe what you said to Clarissa. I'm so disappointed in you.' I looked to the ground.

Ba appeared with two trays of garlic king prawns, shells still on. Their forlorn black eyes bulged, and their long pink antennae bobbed about as Ba walked.

'Where did Clarissa go? I've cooked all of these for them.'

'She went,' said Ma, edging her way past Ba and heading downstairs. She was upset that I had caused her to lose face.

'Who is going to eat these then?' he said, staring at me.

'Nai Nai and I will eat them,' I said. Ba passed me the trays, grateful that his cooking was not going to be wasted.

'Your ma will be okay. She doesn't realise that Clarissa can never be pleased. But she won't hear it from me. Or from you. She has to see it herself, in her own time.'

'Thanks, Ba,' I said.

I walked into the living room. Nai Nai was on the sofa – she turned off the TV when she saw me.

We sat in silence, peeling the prawns and making a big pile of pink shell pieces in the middle of the table. They were juicy and really garlicky – just how I liked them. Even though Nai Nai couldn't speak back to me, I felt like she understood that I wanted to be me: Danny Chung. I desperately needed someone I could talk to. My fingers were greasy so I couldn't draw this time, but just talking would help me feel less guilty about what had just happened. I'd blown up, but it wasn't just because of the Yees – it was everything. Nai Nai nibbled a piece of fried garlic off one of the prawns.

'It's not that I was making stuff up Nai Nai – you know how they are. Every single visit Auntie Yee makes me feel small.' I held up a prawn I'd just deshelled. 'Imagine this is me. I've got no shell, no protection, I'm defenceless and Auntie Yee is like a big shark who is always out to get me.' I bit the prawn in half. Nai Nai smiled and did the same to her prawn.

'Hao chi . . . hao chi.' *Delicious*.

Ba popped his head around the living room door. 'You okay?' he asked.

'Yeah, fine. I think I need some fresh air,' I replied.

'Well, if you're going out, you can take Nai Nai to Mr Potempa's. She wanted you to help her carry some watermelons and more lychees home.'

'Sure. Come on, Nai Nai, let's go,' I said.

19

Eureka!

The Global Mini Mart was looking especially tidy that day. Mr Potempa had arranged the fruit and veg outside in a rainbow arc with reds at the top, followed by orange produce like butternut squashes and satsumas. Bananas and lemons followed, then green, blue and purple fruit were at the bottom. In the middle of the green row was the fantastic spiky veg that we'd seen on Nai Nai's first visit to the shop. I picked it up and started to feel its pointy edges. Nai Nai took it from me and put it in her basket. She gave me a wink and I smiled. It was as if a broccoli and cauliflower had had a baby that had been injected with some weird substance. That is what you would get.

The sign reminded me: Romanesco cauliflower. I loved it. I was so glad she was going to buy it this time. I was sure it would inspire me to draw something very creative.

Mr Potempa appeared in the doorway with his broom. 'Afternoon, Danny and Danny's grandmother. I see you are going to buy one of the special cauliflowers today. Also I have a discount on apricots.'

We went in and walked around the store. Nai Nai chatted away to herself, feeling at home, and began to try a few samples before choosing what to buy. Then we headed home, our arms weighed down with fresh fruit and veg.

After unpacking the bags and filling up the fruit bowls, we sat at the dining table. Ba came to sit down next to us.

'Ma reminded me you have a maths project to do, and that Amelia is in the same competition. Whatever happens, just try your best.'

'Yeah, but I can't think of an interesting area of maths to present on. It's got to be fun and entertaining. It's just, to me, maths is hard and I like drawing.'

'I know you like drawing, Danny, but you need to focus on other things too.' Nai Nai was watching us talk. She said something to Ba and he said something back. 'Nai Nai said maths is a state of mind. And there is always a way through.' Ba looked as confused as I felt.

'Anyway, I need to go break some eggs! Dinner in thirty minutes, okay? You'll figure it out. Maths is in our blood, remember!'

What I needed to do was draw. I was feeling overwhelmed and stressed that I hadn't even begun my maths project. *Maths was in our blood?* The only thing in my blood was platelets. Sitting down at the table with my sketch book and pen made me feel calm. Scanning the room, I looked for inspiration. What should I draw? Nai Nai's funny cauliflower was sitting right in front of me in the fruit bowl like a pointy beacon. Why not?

I began with the outline of the strange vegetable. My pencil zoomed all over, a jagged bit here, a spiky bit there. The word that kept popping into my head as I was sketching was **ALIEN** – it looked like it was extraterrestrial. **THE VEGETABLE FROM OUTER SPACE**. I drew some moons orbiting around the edges of the paper. A little Martian with spring-onion antennae flew around on a turbo-charged mushroom.

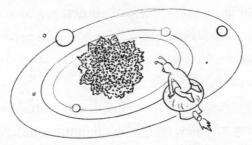

Nai Nai glanced over my shoulder. Then I heard her go 'Ah!' I turned to see what she was doing. Her eyes were the size of dipping bowls and she was pointing to my drawing.

'What is it, Nai Nai?' I asked. She seemed really into my sketch. I felt proud that she was showing so much interest in my work. She started waving her hands as if she had won at bingo. I was confused – my sketch wasn't THAT good, was it? She grabbed the Romanesco cauliflower from the fruit bowl and laid it in front of me, pointing at it as though it was some magical object. She kept jigging about as if she literally had ants in her Ant Gran pants.

'Danny-Ah!!!' She kept tapping the drawing.

'Cauliflower?' I asked. 'What are you trying to say?'

Nai Nai grabbed my maths textbook from my school bag and rushed through the pages. She was searching for something. What was Nai Nai trying to tell me? Then she found it. The page said:

Fibonacci – Maths in Nature

On the page was a picture of the Romanesco cauliflower, as well as other plants and flowers. The text explained how maths was all around us, even in nature. Nai Nai tapped my sketch book and then my maths book, then brought her hands together very slowly in front of me and criss-crossed her fingers. Together? Bring together?

'Integrate them? Maths and drawing?'

Nai Nai wrote down the Fibonacci sequence for me so I could copy it down. It was a series of numbers: 0, 1, 1, 2, 3, 5, 8, 13, 21, 34 . . .

I could see that it's quite simple when you think about it. The next number is found by adding up the two numbers before it. It gets bigger and bigger the more you add. Then Nai Nai drew a grid that showed how it would look when we made squares with those widths, and how you can keep expanding it and expanding it. Then with a blue pen, she traced a spiral.

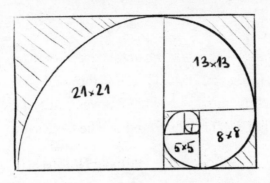

I was loving it; yes, I, Danny Chung, was enjoying something related to maths. Nai Nai picked up the cauliflower again and showed me how each floret was like the spiral pattern, because the florets have to turn and create new turns. It keeps going and going, creating a beautiful thing.

My maths textbook showed a sunflower, and the way its seeds had a similar special formation. I sketched that too.

My mind was full to the brim with ideas of what I could draw and what I could say.

Nai Nai patted me on the back. I stood up and gave her the biggest hug EVER!

'Thanks, Nai Nai. We are a good team after all. Lucky dragons!'

20

Memories of a Lifetime

Nai Nai and I spent the rest of the evening researching other things in nature that used the Fibonacci sequence. For the first time in ages, I felt like I could really do something great. I had a new formula to work with:

My drawing skills + Nai Nai's big maths brain = a cool maths presentation

Perhaps I could DO maths after all.

'Nai Nai, this has been the weirdest few weeks,' I said to her. 'Me and Ravi have fallen out. Carter and his crew were just using me. Ma was trying to make me be like Amelia, and I'm a big disappointment to her. And my room, which I thought was going to get a cool makeover, was somewhere I had no privacy. But right now, you're the only one who accepts me as I am. Ma and Ba never have time for me and are always working. It's just too much, you know?'

'Danny-a. Hao hao-a.' She looked into my eyes and then patted my shoulder, before beckoning me into the bedroom. I got up and followed her. She stood on the chair and pulled her suitcase down from on top of my wardrobe. She laid it on the floor and unclipped it. Inside was a large tatty envelope; the corners were ripped and it had some Chinese characters on it. Sitting on the floor with her legs wide, she poured out the contents. It was a stack of old photos – mostly black-and-white ones, a few in colour. Some had been damaged by age – the sides were brown and gnarly. There were also some papers.

She picked one photograph up and gave it to me to look at. There was a man. He was sitting straight-backed at a table. He held a wooden paintbrush with a soft curved black tip; it looked like very delicate work. Around him were four small pots of ink. He had ears like Ba's. He must be Ye Ye, my grandfather. Ba must have been really upset with Ye Ye because he never had any photos of him at home – I'd certainly never seen one. I liked seeing my grandfather for the first time. Ye Ye had neat hair combed to one side, and I could tell he was very good at concentrating. On the paper in front of him there were bold black brush strokes. I wondered what he was drawing.

Nai Nai showed me a photo of her and Ye Ye with a little baby. 'Ba?' I asked. Nai Nai nodded and smiled. Another one was of Nai Nai and Ye Ye standing in front of a shop counter. There were rows and rows of jars full of small things, perhaps dried fruits. And there was a black-and-white photo of her holding a stick with a silver plate on one end and a weight on the other. That must have been what she used to weigh things. No wonder she was so good with numbers: she had to measure and weigh things every day. Then there was a small framed close-up of Ye Ye – he was smiling directly into the camera, and a young Ba, around my age, was poking his head around Ye Ye's shoulder. They looked happy.

Nai Nai took the photo and held it up in front of her face and then kissed it. She then pressed it to her chest and swayed from side to side. Her eyelids slowly closed. She looked like a little girl who was rocking a doll.

I didn't want to disturb her, so I gently pulled some of the other papers towards me. They were drawings. Well, not drawings like the ones I did. They were paintings. Some with those big black brush strokes I'd seen in the other picture, and some that were more detailed and in colour. Fish swam in small blue ponds; birds flew in cloudy skies; red suns rose above black mountains. Nai Nai had been trying to show me that Ye Ye was an artist too. I was just like him! Ba had always said there was maths in our blood, but he'd never mentioned that there was art too – that I was the grandson of an artist. I wished he had told me more about Ye Ye and why he'd stopped speaking to him.

When I looked up, Nai Nai was crying. Putting down the picture I was holding, I slid across the floor and patted her arm. She wiped her face on her sleeve. I checked for snot, but it was clean.

'Are you all right, Nai Nai?' I asked. I knew I wasn't going to really understand what she would say to me, but when someone is sad you just know. Mr Heathfield said it doesn't take a rocket scientist to know things, which I thought was strange as rocket scientists only know about rockets and science. Did they know how to do a 360 on a scooter or how to make dim sum? They are skills too. I definitely wasn't a rocket scientist, but I knew Nai Nai was sad inside. Sometimes I was sad too. But I hadn't had anyone to tell until now. My sadness must have triggered her sadness, as she was trying to show me something important to her.

'Ye Ye? He's very hao hao.' I felt silly saying *good good*, but I didn't know the right words. He wasn't actually good, was he? He was actually dead. But I wished I knew how to tell her that he looked like a nice guy. She nodded and rubbed her finger over his face. It was good there was glass on there, otherwise she could have smudged the photo with her tears.

Nai Nai started humming a tune. She had put

the framed photo of Ye Ye back in the envelope. Poor Nai Nai, she really had lost a lot of people; her husband and her home country. I was so glad she had Mrs Cruikshanks and, well, us. She needed to get out of the flat and see her friends. She deserved to play bingo and I didn't care what my parents said, I was going to take her there again tomorrow. What they didn't know wouldn't hurt them, as Mrs Cruikshanks had said.

21

Eyes Down

I'd become used to telling small fibs. First with Ravi and then with my parents. But it was for the greater good. Bingo was where Nai Nai needed to be. I might not have any friends right now, but I was determined that she would still have fun.

Nai Nai and I were now pros at sneaking out of the takeaway. We arrived at the community centre in time for bingo. Enid Blue Hair and her special friends were ready with their markers lined up in neat rows. I saw them glancing at Nai Nai as she began to give some people who were sitting by themselves some free fruit. Enid's crew were shaking their heads; their grumbles were low, but it was clear they weren't keen on Nai Nai being her friendly self.

Suddenly, a familiar voice boomed over the airwaves. It was Mrs Cruikshanks – her Scottish accent was unmistakable. 'A wee reminder that bingo is for everyone. Yes, everyone. And I mean black, white, brown, yellow and purple with spots. And while we're on that note – there are NO reserved seats in bingo either. Yes, I'm talking about you, Enid O'Grady.' Some people tutted, while others laughed and nodded their heads. Nai Nai didn't know what the heck was going on, she just saw Mrs Cruikshanks on stage and waved to her with a banana in her hand.

In the background we heard a scuffle and a man's voice: 'Give me that microphone, Nellie, you're not supposed to be up here.'

'Calm yerself down, Tommy, it was a public broadcasting announcement.'

'Hop it!' Tommy said. Mrs Cruikshanks got off the stage and was a bit wobbly when she made her way over to us.

'You made it, Danny! Come on, quick, let's get ready.' She linked arms with Nai Nai and whisked us off to three empty seats in the middle of the hall. I felt odd being the only child in the bingo hall.

'I'm going to stay and watch if that's all right,' I said to Mrs Cruikshanks.

'Of course, Danny, loads of people bring their carers or relatives. You can get some squash if you want. Tell them I sent you.' I jogged off to get a quick cup of squash then raced back and drank it at Nai Nai's side.

The air felt electrified as we waited for the bingo to start. Even the hairs on my arms were standing on end. Nai Nai was focused. I looked at her eyes; they were staring forward. She was nodding her head as if she was revving her engine. She reminded me of an athlete warming up before a big race. Beside her she had a large green plastic bowl the size of a basin, where she had already plonked lychees, cherries and a kiwi. She'd given Mrs Cruikshanks a plastic bag full of satsumas, and in return Mrs Cruikshanks had spread out a bag of Murray Mints between the two of them. She threw one to me.

'Get yer chops around that, Danny.' She looked around. 'What's keeping them? It's supposed to be time.'

'Eyes down,' Tommy announced. He was a large man with a belly that looked like he was having six babies. His red-rimmed glasses looked like they might slip from his nose at any moment. I bet he felt like a king, high up there on stage. He controlled the magic. He was master of the bobbing balls. He was the bingo god. All these people were his worshippers and I was a curious onlooker. I sucked on my Murray Mint and watched in anticipation.

'Ready?' asked Mrs Cruikshanks. She held up two thumbs to Nai Nai, who responded with her own two upright thumbs. Then Mrs Cruikshanks swung them around to me.

'You ready to see yer nan win?' Mrs Cruikshanks said. I nodded. My belly was fluttering.

Then it started.

The machine was whirling and the balls were jostling about like people looking for a bargain during a sale. I couldn't take my eyes off them. In that glass tank was the promise of a token here, a prize there. Anyone could win. It was luck which numbers came up, but it took skill to play multiple cards at once and keep up. Mrs Cruikshanks was right, you could be any kind of human and still win at bingo. It was a game of equals. No wonder Nai Nai loved it. She had found her calling. Her bingo . . . calling.

A green ball was sucked up the tube.

'And the first ball is two fat ladies . . . eighty-eight.' The number appeared lit up on the screen. Nai Nai stamped one of her cards.

'Ba ba . . . hao, hao.' She nodded. I could see a good start was making her feel confident. Eights were considered very lucky in Chinese culture.

'Is she singing "Baa Baa Black Sheep"?' asked Mrs Cruikshanks, not looking at me, her marker pen poised.

'No . . . ba means eight. It's very lucky for her.'

'But I thought Ba meant dad?'

'Yes, well, it does. But it's a different tone. It's complicated to explain.'

'Too bloomin' right. You Chinese come here, speaking your complex language and then learning ours, which is also one of the hardest to learn. No wonder you are all geniuses – you ought to be commended.'

'We're not all geniuses – it's a myth. And I was born here, I didn't come from anywhere but the hospital,' I said, but she was not listening.

'Oh yes! I got that one!' She blotted out a number.

This went on for some time. In between calls, Nai Nai would grab a cherry or a lychee, extract the shell or stalk and suck on it. She'd roll it around her mouth, sometimes storing it in her cheek if she had to concentrate hard.

Looking over at her board, I could see one of her rows was almost complete.

Her foot nearest to me was tapping the floor. She was close and she knew it.

Glancing over, I saw she needed fifty-six.

'Come on, twenty-seven . . . Nellie will be very happy if you showed your face,' Mrs Cruikshanks said.

I squirmed and crossed my legs. Now was not a good time to need the bathroom – it was the most exciting part! Nope, I definitely had to go. I got up and quickly ran to the toilets, which were near the exit.

*

As I ran back into the hall from the toilets, I was expecting to see some lucky person on stage collecting a prize. Instead, there was a commotion. Loads of people had gathered in a bunch near the middle of the hall where our seats were. I couldn't get down the aisles; they were chock-a-block with people.

'What's happened?' I asked as I jostled past an old gentleman with a walking frame.

'Some old biddy called out "bingo" but I think it was too much for her and she collapsed.'

'I think it was that Chinese woman . . .' a voice said.

Nai Nai?

I pushed my way through the crowd.

'I need to get through!' I shouted. 'My grandmother! Let me through.'

When I made it past everyone in my way, I saw that Nai Nai's chair was empty.

Where was Nai Nai?

Was it her who had collapsed?

Had she . . . ? Had she died?

This was all my fault. I had encouraged her to come here. I looked around and finally saw Nai

Nai. She was kneeling on the floor. She didn't look ill – just sad. She was holding Mrs Cruikshanks's hand. It was Mrs Cruikshanks who was lying on the floor, her face very pale.

Nai Nai was chatting away to Mrs Cruikshanks, whose eyes had closed. I could see her cardigan moving up and down so I knew she was alive. She was gripping her bingo card in one hand and a marker pen with the other.

'I'm calling 999! Be quiet, you lot!' shouted Linda, the manager.

I bent down and put my hand on Nai Nai's back. She turned to face me; her eyes were wet.

'Dan Dan,' she said. 'Ah-ya. Nellie.' She held her hand out to me and I gently helped her up from the floor. She put her arm around my middle and gave me a squeeze. I was so happy it wasn't Nai Nai down there. Not just because I would be in the worst trouble in history, but also because I was really starting to like her. And, dare I say it, I even loved her. When someone had said they thought it was the 'Chinese woman', I'd almost cried. But poor Mrs Cruikshanks. I hadn't seen anyone ill like that before. Nai Nai kept her eyes on her friend.

Tommy, the bingo caller, was standing on stage with his microphone. 'Everyone stop being nosy parkers. Nellie needs some space!' his voice boomed through the speakers.

'An ambulance is on its way. We'd be very grateful if you could all make your way outside. Someone, please bring Nellie's bag here,' Linda said, still with her phone to her ear.

'This is all very inconvenient,' said Enid. I felt my palms bunch up and I was about to say something, but then the exit doors burst open and two paramedics arrived.

Linda was standing on tiptoes to see over the heads of the crowd. 'Over here!' She waved at them.

'Come on, Enid, let's go to the cafe and have a cup of tea. We'll come back tomorrow for the Grand Bingo Prize. I'm sure it'll all be back to normal then,' her husband said. Typical – all Enid and her husband did was think about themselves, not Mrs Cruikshanks and how ill she was. The paramedics were quick to check her vitals. A third paramedic wheeled in a stretcher and more equipment. They gently lifted her onto it and tucked her in, pulling up the metal bars on the side. One of them covered her nose and mouth with a clear plastic mask attached to an oxygen tank. Tommy grabbed Mrs Cruikshanks's bag from the table and, as the stretcher passed, he carefully tucked it under the blanket.

Nai Nai moved back to where we'd been sitting. Loads of Mrs Cruikshanks's stuff was still on the table – Tommy had forgotten all of her favourite things. Her picture of Jesus, her cat cushion and her special markers were all still lying there with some mints, satsumas and a half-eaten teacake. Nai Nai picked up my backpack from the back of her chair and began to put Mrs Cruikshanks's things inside, but she left the teacake. Her own bag was full to the brim with fruit. Nai Nai and I headed out of the exit doors, carried along like flotsam on a sea of bingo regulars.

When we got outside Nai Nai kept pointing at the ambulance as it sped off around the corner. Her eyes were welling up. A man standing next to me tapped me on my shoulder.

'Your laces are undone,' he said, pointing to my trainers.

'Thanks,' I replied, and bent down to do them

up. When I glanced up, Nai Nai was moving away from me. 'Nai Nai, wait a minute,' I called, finishing the knot. I stood up and searched for her in the crowd – but couldn't see her. She'd gone.

I looked left and right. Her familiar headband and massive bag were nowhere to be seen. I couldn't believe it. I'd lost my nai nai.

22

Friends Reunited

My mind was whirling. Nai Nai didn't know many places apart from home, my school, the Global Mini Mart and the bingo hall. She couldn't speak English well enough to make her way to the hospital, could she? How could I have been so silly as to lose my gran? If my parents found out I was not with her, I'd be in massive trouble.

Think, Danny, think! I told myself, but my mind was as blank as a newly wiped whiteboard. I wished Ravi were here. He would know what to do. That's it, I thought. Ravi!

I ran all the way from the Longdale Community Centre to Ravi's house. I was sweating and had a pain in my side by the time I arrived. I rang the doorbell and then put my hands on my thighs to catch my breath. I looked up and saw the front-room curtain twitch.

Then the front door opened and Ravi slid out. He already had his jacket on. I could hear his sisters arguing and Vishal crying – their mum was shouting.

'Ravi . . . look . . . I wanted to say . . .' My heart was thumping in my chest and my hands were clammy. I didn't know if that was due to the running or because I was scared that he wouldn't accept my apology.

'Tell me in a minute. I need to get out of this house, man. It's so loud in there I can't think. Let's go.' He zipped up and shut the front door. We walked down his drive and around the hedge.

'Ravi, I wanted first to say . . .' I had to slow down my words to breathe.

'Why have you run here? Been playing with your new best friends? Blasters and all that?'

'No – no, you were right. They weren't cool at all. I need to say . . . I'm sorry.'

'All right . . .' Ravi looked at the pavement. Then he looked at me. 'I'm sorry too.'

'Truce?' I asked.

'Definitely. I didn't mean to tell Tia that you share a bunk bed with your gran. I was going to tell you after school, but you were with Carter.'

'Well, I was angry at you . . . And I wanted to play blasters . . .' Ravi hadn't done it on purpose to make me look bad. I should have just asked him about it straight away instead of thinking he was a bad friend.

'How was it then?' he asked.

'Well, let's just say that birds of a feather really do flock together. It was like hanging out with a bunch of dodos. You were right. Carter is just as bad as the other two. He didn't care about mutants in my comics or finger-jousting.'

'Man, he's missing out. Your comics are so funny,' Ravi said. It made me feel all warm and fuzzy.

'How about a finger-joust to make up officially?' I asked, raising my eyebrows hopefully.

'Sure.' Ravi grinned and got his index finger out and we circled each other just like old times, trying to jab one another in the side. His arms were much longer than mine and he jabbed me in the ribs.

'Ow!' I cackled. 'Haven't lost it, Sir Ravi.'

'Nope! Still got it. Anyway, how has your Easter holiday been so far?' he said as we got to the bottom of his road.

'That's why I'm here actually . . . it's been intense.' My breathing was almost back to normal now.

'Tell me about it. I've seen way too much of my family this school holidays. You don't look yourself – what's up?'

'Well, Nai Nai and I were at bingo, and Mrs Cruikshanks – she's a customer, but also Nai Nai's only friend here – she collapsed when I was in the toilet.' I couldn't get the words out fast enough. It had all happened so fast.

'Was it because you stank the place out?' He grinned and hit my arm – typical Ravi.

'No, man, it was serious, she properly fell down. Maybe a stroke or something. It was really scary, especially as I thought it was my nai nai at first. They took her off in an ambulance. But then Nai Nai vanished straight after. My parents told me not to take her to bingo, but I did, and now she's gone. I know I've messed up, but I need your help, Rav. I don't know what to do!'

'I think you need to make it up to me big time, Danny Chung.'

'I thought you'd accepted my apology?'

'I did, but I'm gonna milk it. Down on your knees like a plebeian asking a feudal lord for mercy.'

'All right' I said, getting down on my knees, '*I, Danny Chung, of the Lucky Dragon takeaway, hereby offer my sincerest apology to my very best friend, Ravi Sebastian Dalal, otherwise known as Sir Ravi of Longdale. I can't believe I lied to you to hang out with that dodo Carter*. Are we cool?'

'Sure. Okay. You can get up now,' Ravi said, smiling. He held out his fist for me to touch. I bumped knuckles with him.

'I'm so glad we're back together!' I said.

'Me too,' he said. With Sir Ravi by my side I felt more confident about sorting out my mess.

'Let's go find your gran,' Ravi said. 'We can head back to yours first and see if she just went home. Then, if she's not there, we can check the hospital.' I knew he would help me out. And just like that, order was restored. Well, with me and Ravi anyway.

When Ravi and I arrived back at the takeaway there was no sign of Nai Nai. I had hoped she would be sitting at the dining-room table spitting out seeds, but her boots weren't at the bottom of the stairs and it was eerily quiet – no humming, no muttering, nothing. Just then, the kitchen door opened and Ba came out.

'Hi, Ravi, it's been ages,' he said. I'd hoped he and Ma would be out, but no such luck.

The front door jangled and then Ma came in with her arms loaded with shopping bags and behind her was Auntie Yee, who wouldn't look at me; her arms were also full of bags. I wasn't expecting to see Auntie Yee after the last 'incident'. But here she was, still poking her nose in.

'Oh, it's you. Your mother kindly offered to buy me a new bag to apologise for your behaviour last time I was here. Amelia is still upset about what you said about her and she didn't want to come here this time.' Lucky Amelia, I thought.

'Danny, where is Nai Nai? I got her a new pair of slippers in the sale,' asked Ma, looking around.

'Ma . . . Ba,' I said, 'I have to tell you something.'

'Nai Nai's boots are not here. Where is she?' Ma continued.

I looked at Ravi and he nodded.

'I'm sorry! I took Nai Nai to bingo but then the ambulance came –'

'Ambulance?' both of my parents said together. Three sets of adult eyes honed in on me. Ba put his hands on his hips.

'Bingo again? Such a preposterous pastime, so uncultured,' Auntie Yee said. 'I warned you. Now she has had a heart attack.'

'No, Nai Nai hasn't had a heart attack, Mrs Cruikshanks has, or maybe a stroke' I corrected.

'Su Lin, this is exactly –' Auntie Yee began.

'Clarissa, please let Danny speak,' Ma said curtly.

'Yes, Clarissa, please be quiet. It's about my mother,' Ba said. Auntie Yee looked shocked that my parents had told her to pipe down. 'Well, Danny? What happened?' Ba asked.

'I've lost her. She was there one minute, gone

the next.' There was a sharp intake of breath from all three grown-ups in the room.

'Lost her? Lost my mother?' Ba repeated.

'I know I'm the worst grandson in the world . . . but . . . let me make this right. I'm sure I can find her. It's the least I can do.'

'Yes, Mr and Mrs Chung, I'll help', said Ravi, backing me up. 'We know our area like the backs of our hands. I'm sure we can find her. 'We can make a list of all the places that Ant Gran – I mean, Danny's gran – would know. She can't have gone that far – Longdale is not that big.'

'Terrible idea,' Auntie Yee proclaimed.

'It is not,' I said. 'I've taken her around this whole Easter holidays and I am the one who lost her. I have to be the one who finds her. Plus, the takeaway opens soon, Ma, so you and Ba have to be here.' I had to convince them to let me do this without them. It was my fault that Nai Nai was missing.

'I think it's a mistake, but what do I know?' said Auntie Yee, looking at her nails.

'No, I think Danny's right,' Ma countered. 'As long as you stay together, okay?' Ravi and I nodded. 'You're right, we do have to be here.

There's a big order coming in at six tonight and we open in forty-five minutes. I haven't got time to go look for her myself and then be back to do the counter.' Ma looked to Ba, who was still thinking.

Ba put his hand on my shoulder, then he nodded. 'All right. Danny, I'm trusting you to handle this and find your nai nai before it gets dark. She knows her way around in the daylight, but things look different at night.' No Chinese Way lecture from Ba? What was going on? I realised there'd been fewer of them since Nai Nai had moved in.

Auntie Yee looked at me and Ravi and made a face.

'I'd call the police if I were you, Su Lin. She's vulnerable,' she said, rummaging in her bag. She pulled out her mobile. 'I would try to find her myself, but I need to get back to Amelia; she's got her piano lesson this evening. Adrian is with her now, helping her with her maths project.'

But something had changed. My mum wasn't taking the bait this time. 'No, Clarissa, we trust Danny. He says he can find her, and we have to give him that chance.' She smiled at me.

'Yes, go bring my mother back home,' Ba said. And with that, he turned and walked into the kitchen.

Ma grabbed two bags of prawn crackers and handed them to me and Ravi. 'Put these in your bag – you'll be missing dinner.'

My bag. Where was my bag?

'What's wrong?' Ravi asked. 'What's the matter? Why'd you look like a zombie?'

'Nai Nai has my backpack. And it has my sketch book in it . . .' Ravi stared at me with wide eyes. He knew what she'd find if she opened the sketch book. I grabbed his jacket sleeve.

'Oh my. She's going to see my **ANT GRAN, SUPERVILLAIN** comic.'

Ant Gran swallowed by a lion mutated with a poodle.

Ant Gran flung into a black hole.

Ant Gran being squished by a giant clown shoe with menacing eyes.

Ant Gran catapulted into the sky by a trebuchet and eaten by the druckon. Quack.

That last one was Ravi's idea.

I had to find Nai Nai before she looked at my comics.

I felt as if I was going to throw up.

23

Lost and Found

We ran to the hospital's A&E department and Ravi told the receptionist that he was a friend of Mrs Cruikshanks's family. They told us what ward she was in, and a nurse walked us down to the middle of the ward, between rows of beds, and pointed to a bed at the far end.

'Visiting finishes in fifteen minutes though, for teatime,' the nurse said.

We carried on walking by ourselves.

'What does she look like?' Ravi whispered.

'Scottish white lady with curly grey hair, a few whiskers, thick brown glasses . . .' I recounted. 'Maybe about ninety-five?'

'I can hear you, Danny! You cheeky blighter. I'm only in my seventies! I'm in here!' Mrs Cruikshanks's voice boomed from behind a curtain.

We hurried over to the cubicle and pulled the blue curtain aside. Mrs Cruikshanks was strapped to a machine and she had tubes going into her nose.

'Are you okay, Mrs Cruikshanks?' I said.

'I've been better. I had a mini stroke, they said. I prefer Mini Cheddars! Flipping bingo was nearly the end of me.' She waved her hand at Ravi. 'Hello, Danny's pal. I've a dodgy ticker, thought my time had come. But Him up above had other ideas – it was not my day to go meet my maker, no, sir.'

'Look,' said Ravi as he bent down to pick up my backpack from the floor. It was open.

'Your wee nan brought me my Lord and my comfy cushion.' Her cat cushion was propping up her back.

'Yes, about her. Do you know where she might have gone?'

'She's upset, Danny. She saw your pictures.' Mrs Cruikshanks picked up my sketch book from the side table and opened it to a page covered in Ant Gran, Supervillain drawings. 'Not very nice, are they? You've broken her heart.'

My chest felt tight.

'I'm sorry that happened, I really am. I didn't mean to hurt Nai Nai's feelings,' I said, and I meant it. I seemed to have got really good at hurting people lately. It made me feel terrible.

Ravi looked at me. His eyes grazed the ground. He'd written some of the speech bubbles.

'It wasn't just Danny – it was me too. We didn't mean any harm. I'm sorry too.'

'Well, it has hurt her . . . hurt her a lot. I am disappointed in you, Danny. I thought you were a good 'un.'

'I know . . . I was wrong to do these. Do you know where she is?'

'I don't. All I know is that she left here with tears in her eyes. Tears. I'll not be surprised if she's lost her winning mojo after this. The Grand Bingo Prize is on tomorrow and I was sure she was going to win it. I haven't seen someone as fast as her in donkey's years.' Mrs Cruikshanks looked very pale. 'Anyway, go and tell one of the nurses I want a cup of tea, will ye?'

We left the hospital with my backpack and a leaflet about the Grand Bingo Prize that Mrs Cruikshanks had given us.

'Where to next?' Ravi asked.

'She loves fruit. Maybe she went to buy some from Mr Potempa?'

We ran down the high street, down the alleyway that led to where Mr Potempa's fruit and vegetable displays brightened up the pavement.

'Hi, Mr Potempa, I was wondering if my grandmother had been in here to buy any fruit today?'

'Yes, Danny, she did come in earlier. She bought masses of produce. Enough for two whole weeks by my calculations. Is she having bowel issues again?'

'No – no – I don't know. Look, we need to find her.'

'Did she say where she was going?' interrupted Ravi.

'Not in any language I have learned!' Mr Potempa said, and he chuckled.

'But did she look okay?'

Mr Potempa stood up and adjusted some soon-to-be-out-of-date packets of Bombay Mix on the counter. 'Danny, I am not in the business of psychological evaluation, my friend. She looked like she needed some fruit to sweeten her up, yes, but then I don't like to get involved in my customers' personal lives. You know how it is. Small talk, yes; large talk, no. I'm too busy running a business for large talk.'

Ravi had wandered towards the chocolate rack.

'She got out her free bus pass and was waving it towards the street,' said Mr Potempa. 'I think she was asking me where the nearest bus stop was. The closest bus to here is the inner-circle one.'

'Okay, she got herself to the hospital, so where is she trying to get to now?' I wondered.

'Okay, thanks, Mr Potempa. What time was that?' asked Ravi.

'About twenty past four. I hope you find her . . . And Danny –'

'Yes?'

'She bought some plums and all of my lychees. A whole bag.' He waved goodbye as we left his store.

Ravi and I started to walk down the high

street in the hope of finding her.

'She can't be far. I mean, a whole bag of lychees is going to be heavy,' I said.

The high street was still busy despite it being near closing time for the shops. The light was beginning to fade. Ravi was really getting into the role of granny-finder; he was going from one person to the next asking in his most serious voice: 'Chinese granny! Has anyone seen a Chinese granny?' I wondered what people would think. He'd taken to the quest quite well.

I gently patted him on the arm and asked, 'Ravi, do you think people will take you seriously if you are shouting that?'

'I dunno, I thought it might help.'

'Okay, I guess it's better than not saying anything.'

I joined in too.

'Chinese granny missing! Reward of free prawn crackers! But don't tell my parents! Chinese granny in exchange for free food. Again, don't tell my parents.' We were like town criers with no bell.

After five minutes of asking about possible

sightings, we decided to give up on that tactic as our throats were beginning to hurt. We trudged around for ages, peering into the row of charity shops that lay back from the main road. I had to stop Ravi from browsing through the piles of old DVDs that they put in boxes outsides. We jogged towards the park. My feet were aching and time was running out.

'I think I'd better go home and tell my parents I can't find her,' I said, feeling defeated. Where would an old Chinese lady with a bag full of lychees go on a Friday evening if she wanted to be alone? I had no idea. My belly made a gurgling sound.

'Maybe we would be able to think more clearly if we had something to eat? I'm kinda hungry now and, from the sounds of it, so are you. Could we have a teeny-tiny break from the search?' asked Ravi.

'All right, but only for a short while,' I replied. We stood outside Chicken Licken.

'I'll get us some chips and a drink,' Ravi said. I passed him a couple of pounds.

'Good idea. Thanks.' I looked at all the people passing by. Nai Nai wasn't anywhere.

Ravi went in and soon appeared with two cones of chips and two cans of pop protruding out of his jacket pockets. We sat down on a bench and began to eat.

'Hey, thanks for coming,' I said, wiping my fingers on my jeans.

'It's all right,' Ravi said. 'It's been quite the adventure, and so not boring or loud like my house.'

Oh no! I grunted and started bobbing my head to one side, trying to say, *Look over there*, without bringing attention to myself.

'Are you okay, Danny? Why are you doing that with your head? Do you want more chips?' Ravi said, offering me his cone.

'No . . . it's Carter,' I whispered. 'He's over there.'

Ravi turned and saw Carter, Mitchell and Jay Jay heading towards us, blaster guns in hand. Carter was wearing a navy baseball cap. As he loomed closer, I could see that it said 'TAKE NO PRISONERS' on it.

Ravi crumpled his empty cone up. I stood and did the same. He took the trash from my hands and went to drop it into the bin a few metres away. I was hoping he was going to be back before Carter reached us.

'Well, well, well . . . if it isn't the Danny who loves his granny,' said Mitchell. It was his attempt at being a poet.

Ravi returned from the bin – his thumbs were hooked into his jacket pockets. His face looked odd.

'Yeah,' said Jay Jay.

'Carter, lads, this is not a great time. Look, I'm sorry I –' I began.

'Chung, you're gonna get it,' said Mitchell, pointing his blaster at my face. Carter laughed.

I really hoped Ravi had his running shoes on. We stood close to one another, our arms touching.

'Boys, boys. No need for that. Danny can't help it if he's poor and has to share a room with his gran. He can't help it that he lives in a flat. Remember, Danny, I told you – make an enemy of me and that's it,' Carter said, bits of spittle hitting my face.

'Loads of people live in flats,' said Ravi. 'There's nothing wrong with Danny's flat.'

'It's okay, Ravi,' I said, patting his arm.

'Carter . . .' I said, not knowing what was going to come out of my mouth.

'Yes, Danny?' he asked.

'Erm . . . well, you see, the thing is . . . I couldn't have helped you even if I had wanted to. I'm no good at maths.'

'I don't believe you,' Carter said. He held up his free hand as if to say, *Enough talking*. Slowly he pointed his blaster at me.

'Danny, be prepared to be pelted. You have five seconds. Then it's your turn,' Mitchell said, looking up at Ravi.

Behind him I could see a double-decker bus moving towards us. I glanced at the top windows. Then I blinked and looked harder. I couldn't believe my eyes. It couldn't be . . . it was Nai Nai! She was on the top deck, right at the front!

'Excuse me, Carter, but I've got to get THAT bus,' I said, pointing to the inner-circle bus, which basically went round and round in a big loop.

'You ain't going anywhere,' said Mitchell.

'Ravi, she's on the bus,' I whispered.

The bus was almost at the bus stop, which was behind Carter and his gang. I'd have to run about five metres to catch it. It was going to be tricky getting past them, but we had to do it, otherwise Nai Nai was just going to end up going round in another circle, and that was going to be my fault too. We'd have to wait another half an hour for the bus to come around again.

'Let us pass, Carter,' I said.

'You're free to go,' he replied, and his smirk made me want to draw him as my next evil villain.

'Get ready,' whispered Ravi.

Ready for what?

To run?

To be blasted in the face by Carter and his gang?

I had no clue what he was on about.

'One, two, three – go!' Ravi ran towards the three boys with his arms outstretched. He started to shriek like a banshee on E-numbers.

'Cooookkkkkkcuuuuuu!!!!' He started to finger-joust them – they didn't know what was going on. Carter's eyes widened. They'd never seen Ravi like this. I'd never seen Ravi like this. Watching Vishal's karate lessons had paid off! Ravi quickly reached into his pocket and pulled out a can of pop, shaking it hard as he ran and shouting, 'Get on the bus!' His pop grenade exploded all over the boys. They didn't know what had hit them! It was wet and cherry-flavoured. Then he got another one out and doused them even more. Sir Ravi of Longdale – my hero! I'd never seen him stand up to them before.

I legged it as hard as I could. I passed the four of them and waved at the driver as he was about to shut the doors. He pushed a button and they opened for me. I dragged myself on. My chest was hurting so bad, like a massive boot had kicked me. I fished in my pocket for some coins and dropped them into the pay box. Turning to see what was happening outside, I saw Ravi running away from the bus, waving at me – then he put his two thumbs up as he weaved through the people on the high street.

Holding tight onto the banister, I made my way upstairs to face Nai Nai.

24

Ant Gran, Superhero!

Nai Nai looked very small sitting on the front seat. Even smaller than usual. Next to her was a large plastic bag with lychee branches sticking out of it. She didn't turn. She just stared forward. Breathing to calm myself, I sat down on the seat next to her, placing my backpack on the floor at our feet.

'Nai Nai, I'm sorry,' I said. She didn't move. Her eyes remained looking forward. 'Nai Nai, I'm sorry I drew those pictures of you.' Still nothing. 'It's true, I was angry at first that I had to share my bedroom with you. It's not easy being eleven. And I . . . well, I know I complain about my chores and stuff. But school is hard when all the others

look like they are having more fun than you . . .
I mean, me.'

Thinking about how she must have felt made
me tear up a little. My eyes were starting to get
wet.

'Nai Nai, I'm really sorry!' I said, leaning over
towards her. I wrapped my arms around her and
lay my head on her shoulder. She patted my back.
I didn't mean to make her cardigan wet – I wiped
my snot off her with my sleeve.

'Hao. Hao. Dan Dan.' She was talking to me.
She leaned over and gently took my backpack
from the floor.

She pulled out my sketch book and flicked it to
a drawing of Ant Gran being tossed into the jaws
of the druckon.

I took the book and ripped out those pages,
tearing them to pieces. She turned to me; the
whites of her eyes were red. She wiped her nose
on a hanky. I began to scribble. I was working so
fast, but I knew exactly what I wanted to draw. A
new Nai Nai comic strip – one that she would be
proud of. When I had finished, I laid it in her lap.

I pointed to where I had sketched her with a
cape and a massive N on her chest.

SUPER NAI NAI – BINGO CHAMPION

Although I wasn't sure she would appreciate me drawing her with her flowery knickers on the outside of her tights, she didn't seem to mind. She stared at the drawing. It felt like ages before she turned to me.

'Nai Nai ai Dan Dan,' she said. *Love*. She still loved me even though I'd been the worst grandson ever, by writing mean things about her and then trying to ditch her at bingo so I could have fun.

'I love you, too, Nai Nai. I have been silly.' I patted my chest. 'Me – Dan Dan – silly.'

She nodded. At least we agreed on something. I remembered that we needed to get off the bus and I knew what would do it. I handed her the leaflet Mrs Cruikshanks had given me.

'Your friend, Mrs Cruikshanks, is okay. She gave me this. Tomorrow you want to go to bingo?'

She scanned the leaflet, and even though I knew she couldn't read the words, she recognised that the numbers meant the prize was a lot of money. She was right, £2,000 was a LOT of money. She sprang up. 'Hao-si!' *House*. She understood. She grabbed her bags of fruit and nudged me out of the way. Then she took my hand and pulled me down the stairs. The bell rang and we got off the bus.

Although Nai Nai had been going round and round on the inner circle, she was now full of beans – or rather fruit. I could smell that she'd had plums and the little *pumpety-pumps* her bottom made told me that she had enjoyed them immensely. Her eyes sparkled with excitement as we headed towards home. It would have to be the last time I ever took Nai Nai to bingo, but it would be worth it. Even if I was grounded for a month. I owed her this.

The bus had gone round in a circle and come back to the high street, so once we'd got off the bus, we saw Ravi running out of a bush next to the bus stop.

'I . . . I . . . held them off as long as I could,' he panted. His body was bent over, his hands resting on his thighs.

'Are you all right?' I asked.

'No,' he managed to say. 'Stitch, arghh!' He stood up and put his hands on his sides.

Nai Nai opened her handbag and rummaged around. She pulled out a small jar.

'Tiger Balm,' I said.

She took Ravi's hand and splodged a dollop on his finger.

'Rub that into your side. It should help with the pain,' I said.

Ravi lifted the side of his shirt and rubbed it in.

'Hot, hot,' he said. 'No, it's actually feeling better.'

He bowed to Nai Nai like she was the queen.

Just then Carter and his crew sprang out of the bushes, blasters at the ready.

'Well, well, well,' said Carter. He was a little out of breath, but the determination to inflict pain was still there.

'Look, he's got his little granny with him.' Jay Jay laughed. I moved in front of Nai Nai so that if they did start shooting, they wouldn't hit her.

'She's sooooo sweet, with her little bags and her woolly hat. She looks like an elf,' said Mitchell.

'Don't you talk about my gran like that,' I said.

'What you gonna do, nana's boy?' taunted Mitchell.

'You're so unfortunate, Danny. I could have made you into one of the coolest boys in the class. Instead, you hang out with these two losers,' Carter said, aiming his gun at my chest. Mitchell was aiming at Nai Nai and Jay Jay at Ravi.

I leaned back into Nai Nai, feeling for the plastic bag in her hand. I grabbed it and swung it towards the ground in front of us. Dropping down, I gathered a handful of lychees and started chucking them at Carter. One hit him dead on the nose. I quickly took aim and threw three more. They hit him in the eyes.

'OW! Ow! Get them!' he shouted to his cronies.

However, before Jay Jay or Mitchell could shoot, Nai Nai had swooped forward and grabbed a bunch of the hard, spiky-skinned fruit and begun to lob them at Mitchell like a baseball pitcher. Her aim was magnificent. She hit him in all types of places, especially places that hurt boys. Ravi got in on the action and soon the place was covered in the brown and red shells – some had cracked open and a carnage of white slime balls littered the pavement.

Mitchell turned and ran away.

Carter grabbed Jay Jay and ducked behind his smaller friend.

'Get off me, Carter! Let me go!' Jay Jay obviously didn't appreciate being used as a human shield. He wriggled and squirmed out of Carter's grip and followed in the direction that Mitchell had fled. One of them had left a blaster on the floor in the commotion.

Ravi walked over and picked it up.

'Be a shame to leave it here,' he said. He held it to his chest.

'HAO-SI!' Nai Nai said, and she picked up the bag of the remaining lychees.

25

Cyborg Devil Rebellion

Today was the day! The Grand Bingo Prize was being held at Longdale Community Centre at the usual time of 2 p.m. Ravi had come over to offer moral support. He sat next to me on the sofa as we watched Nai Nai.

'Does she always walk up and down like that?' he asked, watching Nai Nai pace the living-room carpet.

'Not normally,' I said. Nai Nai kept looking at the clock.

'Did you absolutely promise your parents not to take her to bingo ever again?' Ravi asked.

'I did promise, but I guess it wasn't an

"absolute promise",' I said, trying to think of ways I could get out of it. Nai Nai had been there for me when I needed someone to help me and she had stood up to Carter yesterday. She was part of our team now. It wasn't just me and Ravi any more. Nai Nai was an honorary member of our gang and she deserved to go to that bingo tournament. I watched as she kept picking up the leaflet and then putting it down. She glanced at the clock on the wall as the time ticked closer and closer to game time.

'We've got to take her,' I said to Ravi. 'We just need to get out of here without being noticed.' I sat on the edge of the sofa and began scribbling a note to my parents. Just then, the living-room door opened and Ma entered, followed by Auntie Yee and Amelia. Auntie Yee was wearing a lilac dress, and Amelia was in jeans and a grey sweater. It was the first time I had seen her looking different to her mother, no colour co-ordination whatsoever! It was a Cyborg Devil rebellion.

I was still wary of her though so I slid the note down the side of the sofa into the cushions. I motioned to Ravi with my eyes to hide the Grand Bingo Prize leaflet that was on the coffee table in the middle of the room. He started to do weird stretches, as if he had just got out of bed. Amelia frowned when she saw him. He did a side lunge and knocked the leaflet off the coffee table, out of sight.

Amelia was sulking. 'But do I have to stay here? Why can't I just stay at home with Daddy?'

'I told you, he's coming with me and we won't have room in the car for the new mirror if you are there too – we need to put down the back seat. I can't have a cracked mirror in my bedroom. It's bad luck.'

'It's no problem,' said Ma. 'You can stay all afternoon if you like, Amelia.'

'That won't be necessary, Su Lin. Just an hour will suffice,' Auntie Yee said.

'We'll be quick,' said Uncle Yee, who appeared behind them all. 'We'll pick up the new mirror, drop it home and then come pick you up and take you to your conservatoire audition,' he said, looking at his daughter.

Amelia walked over and sank into the sofa. The note was sticking up next to her.

'Thank you, Su Lin. Please be mindful of Amelia's braces – no food that might get clogged up. Amelia, be ready at two on the dot, as we can't miss the appointment with the conservatoire – we've waited six months.'

I saw Amelia roll her eyes a little and turn her head away from her mother. 'YOU'VE waited six months . . .' I heard her mutter under her breath.

The Yees left and Ma held the door for them. 'Okay, kids, you have fun. Help yourselves to fruit. We have enough to feed a village. I've got to go into the kitchen. No fighting now, okay?' With that, she turned and left the room.

Ravi recognised Amelia from the **CYBORG DEVILS** pictures – braces and all. 'Hi, you must be Amelia, I've heard all about you.' He gave me a big grin.

'Hi,' she said. There was no barb, no sarcastic taunt. What was wrong with her today? 'And you must be the famous Ravi. Danny mentions you all the time.'

I felt a bit weird. Amelia had actually been listening to what I was saying even when she looked like she was ignoring me.

I then watched with horror as she noticed the paper down the side of the sofa. She plucked it out and began to read it.

Dear Ba and Ma,
There is somewhere
that I HAVE to take
Nai Nai today. It's
really important. I'm
sorry! I hope you will
understand.

P.S. I promise not to
lose her this time!

'Where do you HAVE to take your Nai Nai?'
Amelia asked.

I felt my face go red. Amelia could tell on us.
I wasn't sure if I could trust her now. But I had
little choice. She was here and knew all of our
plans.

Nai Nai came over to me and gave me the
leaflet for the Grand Bingo Prize she'd picked
up from the floor. She tapped it. Then pointed
at the clock.

'Hao-si?' she asked.

'Bingo!' Amelia figured out. 'She wants to go
to bingo?'

'She wants to go really badly,' Ravi said.

'We have to take her,' I said. 'But are you going to tell on us?'

'I haven't decided,' said Amelia, getting up from the sofa. She saw Nai Nai with the bingo leaflet. Great, our fate rested in the hands of Amelia Yee. She'd tell her mum, who would tell my parents and all the good stuff I'd done, like finding Nai Nai on the bus, would be for nothing. Nai Nai looked at the clock on the wall. Then she came up to me and took hold of my hand.

'Nellie, Hao-si. Winner.' She patted her chest. My heart exploded. Nai Nai was talking to me and I could understand her. She was so clever and quick. She wanted to win for Mrs Cruikshanks. Amelia was looking at each of us in turn.

'She has to get to bingo. It's her knight-errant quest. I can take her if you want me to?' Ravi offered.

'No, I have to go too. She and I are a team – the Lucky Dragons. I have to be there and support her because Mrs Cruikshanks is still in the hospital. Okay, let's go . . . but –' I turned to stare at Amelia. She would snitch on us for sure.

Amelia bit her lip and then said, 'You can go if you want, I won't tell on you. In fact, can

I come?' I couldn't believe it. Amelia Yee was being . . . nice? She continued: 'This Easter break has been the worst. Extra piano lessons, doing the maths presentation every night – I don't want to meet the Mayor of Birmingham or ride in a limo. I don't want to audition for the Birmingham Conservatoire because then I'll have to practise even more. I just want to do something fun for a change. I promise not to tell, but only if I can come too.' I suddenly felt really sorry for Amelia. Her mum was a beast. And Amelia never talked about her friends, never mentioned anyone by name. At least I had my bestie, Ravi.

I looked at Ravi. He looked at me. We both looked at Nai Nai.

'Okay, we're all going. Amelia too.'

Amelia smiled. She looked actually – dare I say it? – friendly. 'Nai Nai,' I said, turning to my gran, 'come on, we're going to bingo!' I left the note I'd written in the middle of the coffee table. Nai Nai did a little hop and ran to get her bag. She emptied the fruit bowl into it, then we all tiptoed downstairs, put on our shoes and silently left the takeaway one by one. Then together we walked away as fast as we could.

Yes, I would be grounded for life when Ma and Ba found out I had disobeyed them for a third time. But this was bigger than me, it was bigger than Ma and Ba. It was for Nai Nai. It was Nai Nai's Chinese Way! Ma and Ba were always going on about trying our best and succeeding in life. This was Nai Nai's chance to succeed here in a strange land far from her home.

26

And the Winner Is . . .

When we arrived at the bingo, nearly every seat was taken. Everybody wanted to win the £2,000 prize money. We walked in and scanned the room, looking for a good location where we could see the board. There was a seat next to Enid right in the middle of the room, but she quickly put her cardigan on it as we walked by. Nai Nai smiled and I heard a faint sound. I think my gran had farted as she passed by her nemesis.

'No way,' said Ravi. We chuckled and clamped our hands over our mouths and then over our noses. My God, Nai Nai was lethal. Fruit bombs.

Amelia and Ravi helped Nai Nai find a place

to sit near the far wall, and I went to buy her the bingo cards and then went to join them. Enid wasn't the only player to have an entourage. I helped Nai Nai take off her lucky red-and-gold dragon jacket and placed it on the back of her chair. Amelia arranged the cards neatly in front of her. And Ravi massaged Nai Nai's shoulders. She  got out her markers and fruit supplies from her handbag and sat still, with her hand poised. We'd only just made it in time.

The lights went down. The screen turned on and the bingo balls began bobbing in their glass box. Tommy, the bingo caller, was sat in his chair on the stage.

'Welcome everyone to the Grand Bingo Prize. I've heard from the hospital that Nellie is doing well. We're sending you our best wishes, Nellie!'

Many of the bingo players looked relieved.

'Today we have a prize of a whopping two thousand pounds for one lucky winner, kindly sponsored by *Sausages R Us*. The two runners-up will receive a year's supply of sausages. Vegetarian sausages are also available. Are you ready?'

'Yes!' yelled the room.

'Get on with it!' shouted one of Enid's gang.

'Then it's eyes down!' Tommy began.

It was like being in a place where magic happened but you weren't in on the trick. You either had the numbers or you didn't. You either got there fast or you didn't. It was like this was Nai Nai's time, because it WAS her time. It was the most exciting day I'd ever had in my entire life! I held my breath as I watched Nai Nai go to work.

Her hand–eye coordination was impressive. She was concentrating hard but managed to still suck on some lychees. Her marker was blotting out numbers as soon as they were called. The numbers came thick and fast from the popping tube. The caller was eagle-eyed, checking to make sure he had the ball the right way round.

Pop! Pop! Pop!

The machine spat up the rainbow balls one by one. The lights on the screen lit up as each ball was called. Furious hands, wrinkled hands, determined hands all over the bingo hall battered the cards, covering them in pen-splodge measles. It was like the papers had caught a rash. Nai Nai was on fire.

Bam! Bam! Bam! went her marker pen in lucky red.

I peered around the room in anticipation of someone else calling out 'House'. The Grand Bingo Prize would be gone at any moment. I started to jog up and down. It was me who had ants in my pants now.

'God, this is so exciting!' squealed Amelia, hands to her mouth. She was biting her nails anxiously.

'It's like watching a master at work,' said Ravi.

Then I saw them. Ba and Ma's heads passed by the window outside. They must have got the note I'd left. Now they would be able to see how brilliant Nai Nai was at bingo – I was kinda glad to see them here, because she was so close now. Behind them trailed Auntie and Uncle Yee. What were they doing here? It would be a disaster if they caused a ruckus. Nai Nai was nearly there.

'Look over there.' I pointed to the window. Amelia and Ravi turned.

'What shall we do?' I said, panicking.

'Come on, we'll block the doors.' We ran over and held the handles. Linda, the manager, was giving us a funny look. She was heading towards us. Ba's and Ma's heads appeared on the other side of the door. They were in the lobby now, looking in through the window. Then Auntie Yee scrambled to the other window of the door. She was fuming and pointing. We couldn't hear what she was saying, but it was way past two. Amelia had missed her audition at the conservatoire.

'You two hold the doors, I need to check on Nai Nai!' I ran back to where my little gran was working hard. One of her bingo cards was nearly full. It was excruciating. Nai Nai kept sucking on her lychees and, *pow*, the seeds went into the bin without her moving her gaze. She had perfected the side spit.

She only needed the number eight now. Come on, lucky eight!

Linda had asked Ravi and Amelia to move from the exit doors and Ba, Ma, Auntie Yee and Uncle Yee were now in the room. They were scanning the rows of tables, looking for Nai Nai and me. I crouched down, holding Nai Nai's shoulders.

'You can do it, Nai Nai!' I said.

Just then a voice screamed out, 'House!'

It wasn't Nai Nai. I stood up to see who it was.

'Very funny, Barry, you're not even playing!'

shouted Tommy over the microphone. 'Keep those eyes down. Someone get Barry out!' The unfortunate Barry was taken towards one of the fire exits. His mother got up too, and was still marking off her card as she walked backwards.

Ma and Ba were striding now down the middle aisle, but instead of the frowns that I was expecting, they were both smiling. Ba put one arm around Ma as he walked towards us. I could let go of my fears of being grounded forever. Ma pointed to Nai Nai, who was concentrating on the bingo screen, her eyes wide like a tarsier's.

Auntie Yee was jogging in her stilettos towards Amelia, who was standing like a deer in the headlights, unable to move. Uncle Yee already had his hands up in a *nothing-to-see-here* manner.

'Danny, you are such a bad influence on Amelia. We've missed her audition because of you,' Auntie Yee said, poking me in the shoulder. It was a pretty painful finger-joust – those talons hurt.

My parents sped up to reach us. Ba put his arm out as if to say STOP. Ma calmly pulled me towards her, out of Auntie Yee's reach, and then moved in front of me like a human shield. 'Oh no, we don't go around prodding other people's children, Clarissa, that is not on. This is the last time you put my Danny down, so I suggest you find someone else to bully. And take up baking classes while you're at it – your steam cakes taste like rubber.'

It was the first time Ma had really stood up for me. Auntie Yee was speechless – another first. She grabbed Amelia and marched her down the aisle to the exit. Uncle Yee was walking backwards, bobbing his head in apology to Ma. I was so proud of my mum.

'Sorry, Su Lin, she's not been the same since that Women's Society meeting. They judged her cake very harshly. I'll take them home. Apologies, apologies.' Poor Uncle Yee, I thought. But I was glad they were going.

'This is a ridiculous game!' shouted Auntie Yee, trying to get the last word in as always. She was met with a spatter of boos from the regulars. Enid and her cronies stood up menacingly and waved their fists at Auntie Yee as she stumbled out of the bingo hall, declaring everyone in there a 'heathen'. Amelia gave us a thumbs up as she exited the doors, her brace catching the light. She wasn't so bad after all.

'This was awesome! Let's do it again!' she shouted.

I looked at my parents. 'You're not angry?' I asked.

'Well, we found the note and we didn't know what to expect . . .' said Ma. 'Or whether to be cross with you for not listening to us again. But seeing Nai Nai so happy, we can see why you wanted to bring her. She loves it here.' Ba was busy looking at the screen and then scanning Nai Nai's card with his eyes.

Nai Nai was still waiting for the number eight.

Ma put her arm around my shoulders and gave me a squeeze. Ba looked over at Nai Nai's card and then grinned. He knew his mother was on the precipice of greatness.

'Come on, Ma!' he squealed. I'd never seen my dad that excited before.

Nai Nai didn't move, except . . . her ears may have twitched. She had two lychees stuffed into her cheeks. And then it happened. The number appeared on the screen.

8

Nai Nai rose and shouted 'Hao-si!!!' Number eight had saved the day.

She stood up on the table, waving her card – it was fully covered in red dots. Nai Nai scrambled over the table, darted across to the stairs and up onto the stage towards Tommy. We all held our breath. You could have cut the tension with a meat cleaver. I felt a finger-joust in my side rib. Ravi was as nervous as I was.

Linda checked the numbers and then Tommy did a re-check using the screen to mark off the balls on Nai Nai's card. We watched as the numbers on the grid went black. Those were the ones Nai Nai had got.

WINNER!!! flashed in bright pink and yellow on the screen and beneath that: **£2,000!!!!!**

We all collectively exhaled.

'She's done it!' I exclaimed. My face was hurting from the size of my grin. Ravi and I started to jump about on the spot like rabbits who'd overdosed on sugar.

'She's won two thousand pounds?' Ba asked, looking up at his mother dancing on the stage. Ravi and I nodded. Ba began to kiss Ma on the cheek.

'That's my mother! She's a winner!' he started to tell the bingo player nearest him, pointing up at Nai Nai. 'That's MY MOTHER!' he shouted a bit louder.

'We know,' came the deadpan reply of Enid's husband.

I looked up and Tommy was shaking Nai Nai's hand on stage. Nai Nai indicated that we should go up too. Without a second thought, Ba, Ma, Ravi and I all ran up onto the stage and hugged Nai Nai. Our winner.

Linda was there too, holding a massive cheque. 'I'm happy to announce that this lady, Nellie's friend, has won the jackpot! What's your name, love?' she asked. 'I need to fill this bit in.'

Nai Nai shouted 'Hao-si!' again. Ma and I laughed.

'Dong Mei! My mother's name is Dong Mei!' Ba cried out with glee. He spelt out the words for Linda, who wrote Nai Nai's actual name on the giant cheque. 'It means *Winter Plums*,' he added. I'd finally found out my grandmother's name and I couldn't think of one that better suited her.

Tommy announced, 'Dong Mei, also known as Winter Plums, has won this month's Grand Bingo

Prize! Do you have anything you want to say?' He held the microphone out to Nai Nai.

'Hao-si! Winner!' Nai Nai boomed into the microphone. The room erupted, with marker pens being flung down onto tables in defeat. One lady started to applaud and then more joined in. Even Enid's husband began to clap, but his wife slapped his hands.

Most of the room were clapping for Nai Nai. She was officially the best bingo player in the room. Nai Nai kissed Tommy the bingo caller on the cheek. His face went a shade of beetroot. Linda handed Nai Nai the giant cheque for two thousand pounds as well as an envelope with a small one, to pay in at the bank, and Ma and Ba stood next to me with the biggest smiles I'd seen from them in ages.

Nai Nai was on top of the world, holding up a cheque that was bigger than she was.

27

Maths Is Fun!

And that was the day my nai nai from China won loads of money and changed the hearts of many people who weren't used to strangers. She was the bravest person I'd ever met. I mean she'd travelled thousands of miles to come be with us, she couldn't speak the language and didn't know anyone. She deserved more, especially from me. I made up my mind to really appreciate having her in my life. And she was a maths champion after all. I really was a lucky dragon having her in my corner to help me with the thing I was worst at.

We spent the second week of the Easter

holiday working on my maths project. I spent ages creating the most amazing illustrations to show how maths could be found in nature and how Fibonacci aka Leonardo of Pisa, was a proper cool dude for figuring it out.

Back at school on Monday morning after our eventful Easter break, Mr Heathfield pulled out people's names from a hat. The video camera was ready to record all of the presentations, which would then be sent to the mayor's office, where the judging panel would choose the winner. The winning school would be notified once all the entries had been sent in.

Carter's Fortnite presentation was a bit like watching soggy lettuce. I thought it would be exciting, but it was mostly him droning on about how many people he'd hit and the probability of him beating his highest score.

Ravi's hip-hop fractions presentation was sooo awesome. He got the whole class swaying from side to side with their arms in the air. His cousin Deep came in with some turntables and flashing lights like you see at a disco. Ravi wore a knight's helmet and held a foil-covered shield that had loads of circles divided up into sections.

There was a section for how many ogres he'd slain, and how many maidens he'd rescued. I didn't even know Ravi could rap!

'Danny! Your turn,' Mr Heathfield said, giving me the thumbs up. The red light flashed on the side of the camera.

'Yes, sir, a pleasure, sir.' I was grinning. I'd never been so excited to talk about something maths-related in my life. But, to be honest, my topic didn't feel like maths. It felt more like art.

I stood up in front of my class. My hands weren't sweating and I was breathing normally. 'Everyone, I'd like to introduce you to my nai nai – Dong Mei.' I smiled. 'It means *Winter Plums* and I think that's why she loves fruit so much.' I opened the door to the classroom and Nai Nai came in, carrying a basket of vegetables and fruit and my cardboard artwork.

'My maths presentation is about maths in nature and art. A long time ago a man called Leonardo of Pisa came up with the Fibonacci sequence . . .'

Nai Nai held up the large pieces of A3 card I had prepared. I had drawn Leonardo with a long beard, a brown cloth dress and a baseball cap.

I got out a Romanesco cauliflower that Nai Nai had bought from Mr Potempa's and passed it around  the room. I heard 'ahhhs' and 'ohhhs'.

'Whoooaa! What IS THAT?' screeched Tia. I could see that she was well impressed. I let my classmates pass it around the room.

'That's soooo freaky, but I like how it feels,' said Grace as she ran her fingers over the green spikes. 'Can you eat it then?'

'What's this got to do with maths?' Carter said, faking a yawn. I could tell he was jealous.

'Well, as some of you know, maths is not my strongest subject. Despite that, my grandmother here showed me that maths is all around us. We don't need to be afraid of it. It's in nature too.' Ravi gave me a little thumbs-up and a smile.

'I didn't know that,' said Tia.

I went on to show them more sketches of Leonardo's sequence and how the numbers expanded and where you could find them in nature. Nai Nai had saved my bacon.

Even Mr Heathfield was impressed. He clapped

his hands and actually patted me on the back after I'd taken a bow.

'Well done, Danny and, er . . . Danny's grandmother, who I am guessing did not draw these wonderful pictures,' he said. 'Thank you to those of you who presented today. You have blown me away.'

'And I can see you have worked hard on these over the Easter break. They were definitely entertaining and informative. We've filmed them all and will send the best ones to the judges. We'll know by the end of the week who the prize-winner is, and if it's a student at this school, we'll tell you in the school assembly. Good luck, everyone. I'm really proud of you all.'

At the end of the lesson, Mr Heathfield came over to me. He leaned in and said, 'I was really impressed with your drawings and how you thought outside the box, Danny. Keep up the good work. You know you can always come and ask me questions if you don't know how to do something?'

'Thank you, sir. I will,' I told him.

I was sure someone like Amelia Yee would be the winner, as she was always top in everything.

But even if I didn't win, I was happy to have created a great presentation for once. Nai Nai had shown me that, actually, DANNY CHUNG DOES DO MATHS, just in my own way.

On Wednesday, after school, we took Nai Nai to see Mrs Cruikshanks, who was still recovering in hospital. When we told her that Nai Nai had won the prize money and showed her the big cardboard cheque she whooped and cheered, pressing the orange button so she could tell the nurse on duty that her best friend had won this month's Grand Bingo Prize. The nurse fake-smiled and told her the button was for emergencies and assistance only. Mrs Cruikshanks started chanting 'Hao-si! Hao-si! Hao-si!' and soon Nai Nai, Ba and Ma were all doing it too. Ravi and I were trying to suppress our giggles when the staff nurse came and told us to be quiet.

Ba translated for Nai Nai when Mrs Cruikshanks said she was feeling much better and that she was lucky it wasn't a heart attack. It was a mini stroke and hey'd said she could go back home in the morning, and she'd be right as rain in a few weeks.

'I don't know what I'm going to do if I can't go to bingo or do my charity work,' Mrs Cruikshanks said. 'My house is too big just for me. That's why I like to be out and about. To see people and have a natter. How am I going to get my Chinese food if I'm stuck at home?' she asked.

'I can bring you the food,' I told her.

'Ah, you're an angel, Danny,' Mrs Cruikshanks said. 'And did you apologise to your nan here for those pictures you did?'

'I did. It's all fine now, and I even drew her a new comic where Nai Nai was a superhero,' I said.

'I'm glad,' she said. She turned and gave Nai Nai a gummy smile. Her false teeth were in a plastic cup on the bedside table. 'Dong Mei, such a lovely name,' Mrs Cruikshanks said, pointing to the cheque. 'And two thousand pounds is a whopper.'

'Maybe it can help us buy a bigger house,' I said to Ba.

'Danny, Nai Nai would have to win quite a few of those Grand Prizes for us to buy our own place,' Ba said.

'You'll have to keep sharing with her for a while yet,' Ma added.

Mrs Cruikshanks shifted a little more upright. 'I've just had a funny idea. I've got four spare rooms at my home. Two with an en-suite. My kids live in Santa Fe in America, so I never get visitors. Dong Mei can come stay with me if she likes. I've got a garden and you can come over and play any time, Danny, with your friend here.'

Ma looked at Ba, who looked at me, then at Nai Nai. He translated the message from Mrs Cruikshanks to his mother, and Nai Nai's face lit up. She practically beamed. She started talking non-stop and then gave Mrs Cruikshanks a big fat kiss.

'So that's sorted then!' said Mrs Cruikshanks. 'We'll be like *The Golden Girls* on the telly.' I didn't know what she was on about, but Ba laughed, and Ma chuckled, too. Then Mrs Cruikshanks starting singing 'Thank you for being my friend!' while holding Nai Nai's hand.

Ba was sad to see Nai Nai move out, but Ma told him to stop crying.

'She's only five roads away!'

Ba and Ma packed all of her things into the van and we pulled up outside Mrs Cruikshanks's place – it was massive and had five bedrooms. Her children had all moved out and her husband had died totally unexpectedly, a bit like Nai Nai's. No wonder she was out all the time – she was lonely in such a big house. Nai Nai walked up towards her new home at 95, Birch Avenue with a smile on her face, carrying two massive laundry bags full of stuff. Mrs Cruikshanks was standing by the front door, grinning widely, and was holding a banner that had been hastily scribbled with a bingo marker. It said:

WELCOME, NEW ROOMIE!

Finally, the end of the week came around. Friday was the big day – we were going to find out who would spend a day in a limo and go to the Knights of Old theme park. My money was on Amelia or someone from her fancy school. We crowded into the main hall for assembly – the whole school was there. Mr Heathfield was on stage, which was unusual.

We all sat on the floor and looked up.

'Hello, school. Today we've been notified that one of our pupils has won the maths presentation competition for Maths Is Fun. The winner will receive a day in a limo with friends, a meeting with the Mayor of Birmingham and tickets to the theme park Knights of Old.'

'It's not going to be any of us,' Carter said behind me.

Mr Heathfield was smiling. 'I'm more than proud to say that someone in my own class has won and the limo is waiting outside as I speak.' The whole room ohhhed and ahhhed.

'Settle down,' said Mrs Brannan with force from the side of the hall.

Mr Heathfield looked over towards me . . . 'The winner is . . .' No way . . . was he going to say my name? Had Nai Nai's winning touch finally landed on me?

'. . . Ravi Dalal from 6H for his hip-hop fractions!' Ravi looked at me, and I looked at him.

'Yes! Well done, Sir Rav!' I said excitedly. I hadn't come first, but it didn't matter because I got to show that maths wasn't always about doing sums, and I got to draw some awesome stuff too.

'Man! We're going to Knights of Old in a limo!' Ravi said, his grin the biggest I'd ever seen it.

'We?' I said, pretending that I didn't know he would totally be taking his best friend – who is me!

'I can't believe I won something!' he added.

'You deserved it. Your presentation was amazing,' I told him.

I gave him a double fist pump and then finger-jousted him in the side ribs. Mr Heathfield waved his hand urging Ravi to go up on stage to collect the tickets. As he walked, he looked just a little bit taller. His head was held high. He was Sir Ravi of Longdale. Mighty rapper and slayer of fractions. The whole room clapped for him (apart from Carter, Mitchell and Jay Jay who had begun arguing about whose fault it was that they hadn't won). This was the best week ever.

Epilogue

A Room of One's Own

That week, Ba and Ma took a few days off work, which had NEVER happened before, EVER. They said that after seeing Nai Nai and I have so much fun together, they realised they had been missing out.

'We've been working too hard all of these years, Danny, and Nai Nai had only been here a few weeks and understood what you liked doing, and who you were,' said Ma.

'Yes, and I'm going to join a yoga class and take more time off,' said Ba. 'My back pain was a sign that I was overdoing it.'

My parents also said I could have the room

makeover, as they said we weren't going to be moving any time soon. They let me decide what colours to decorate my room, so I chose a colour called 'verte', as it reminded me of the Romanesco cauliflower. It was so much fun choosing how I wanted my room to look. I helped paint the walls and doors. Ma said I did a professional job too. She got me a new set of bedding that matched the walls. And under my window I had a new desk and chair with drawers for my paper and pens. In the corner was a bean bag and a TV on a pull-out bracket. I'd never have to leave my room again if I didn't want to.

The room was now ready for Ravi to come over and have a sleepover! There was no more football duvet, and Nai Nai had taken the orange one with her. And she gave the bobble hat to Mrs Cruikshanks, who wore it every time she went out. It went well with her raincoat.

But the best of all was that I had an ART WALL. I was pinning up some of my drawings when I had visitors.

'Nai Nai and Mrs Cruikshanks are here with a new addition for your art wall,' Ma said. Both women squeezed into my bedroom. Ma and Ba huddled near the window. Nai Nai handed me a large red cardboard box. I ripped it open and it was one of Ye Ye's brush paintings of a dragon. I felt a lump in my throat the size of a lychee and gave Nai Nai the biggest hug.

'Thanks, Nai Nai, I love it,' I said.

Ba came over holding a hammer, put up a hook and hung the picture on it. He straightened it, then he started wiping his eyes. 'Something in my eye, just some dust.' He turned away.

Ma came over then and put her arms around me. 'We love you, Danny, and we want you to know that, with or without a fancy room.'

'Thank you, both of you,' I said. 'It's perfect.' We stood in a row and looked at my new wall of awesomeness. It had my best sketches – **THE DRUCKON, STUNT SNAIL, ANT GRAN, SUPERHERO** and, on the right, my maths presentation certificate. It said my presentation was 'highly commended'. Ba had pinned up my drawings of Leonardo of Pisa, who I discovered did some other cool stuff as well as the Fibonacci sequence, like he helped popularise the numbers we use today instead of Roman numerals.

Maths would be even harder if we all had to use Roman numerals, that's for sure.

'Thank Nai Nai. She insisted she wanted to pay for lots of this new stuff with her bingo winnings.'

'But I thought you hated art because it had no purpose?' I said to Ba.

'I was wrong. Ye Ye was an artist, just like you,' said Ba, 'and he gave up a very good job to pursue his art. I blamed him because we didn't have enough money for me to attend university. I moved here, and we never forgave each other. To me, art didn't have a purpose, it only brought us sadness.' Ba pulled me close and hugged me. 'I'm sorry, Danny . . . for stopping you drawing. It's your gift, I see that now.'

Nai Nai tapped me on the arm, then handed me something long, rolled up in kitchen paper. I peeled open the parcel and inside were some wooden paintbrushes.

'They were your Ye Ye's,' Ba said. He pulled out some blank canvases from behind the door. 'Here, Danny. We want you to do what makes your heart sing,' he said. 'Draw and paint – whatever you do makes us proud.'

I couldn't believe it. No more Chinese Way lectures, no more talks about everything having to have a purpose, no more wanting me to be more like Amelia! I gave my dad the biggest hug. Then everyone else piled on for a group hug.

'This is so emotional,' said Mrs Cruikshanks, wiping her eyes. 'I feel like I've got a family again.'

'Thank you, Nai Nai,' I said, holding up the paintbrushes.

I put my arms around her.

Nai Nai patted my back.

'I love you,' I said.

'I love Dan Dan,' she replied.

A Note from the Author

When I was growing up in our council house in Birmingham, I felt mostly like a regular kid. I didn't know I was 'different' until other people made me feel I was not like them. I spoke like them, I ate the same foods as them, I had pets and played in the park like everyone else. But I remember being around seven and thinking 'Is there is something wrong with me? What is it?'

It was my skin. I didn't look like some people. I was a transracial adoptee and was raised quite 'English' (but we always had other Chinese children and families around when I grew up, so I felt I had some aspects of Chinese culture around me). However, there was part of me that was inherently 'Chinese'. I couldn't escape that even though sometimes I really tried to, which is a little like Danny in this book.

You've heard it all before, that if you don't see yourself in books and on the screen then you don't feel represented. I had exactly that experience. I didn't know who I was. I've written *Danny Chung*

Does Not Do Maths for all of those British-Chinese and British East and Southeast Asian kids who have never seen a kid who looks like them on the cover of a British middle-grade book. AND it's written by me, a person who knows exactly what it feels like to be singled out for looking slightly different, but feels very British inside.

I was inspired by meeting my friend's grandmother who came to live in Birmingham aged 92! I thought, wow, she's moved to a new country at a very ripe age and left behind all she has known. What a brave woman. Her grandchildren couldn't understand her dialect, but loved her all the same. I also wondered what she could do to pass the time and I imagined she could go and play bingo – and that is how Nai Nai, Danny's grandmother, was born. I also met my own Chinese grandmother in my late twenties and even though I didn't speak the same language, we got on very well.

Danny Chung Does Not Do Maths is filled with humour and humanity for these strange and uncertain times. It's a book about belonging and I hope you enjoyed reading it.

Maisie Chan

Acknowledgements

Writing *Danny Chung Does Not Do Maths* was pure pleasure. Parts of it made me laugh even when I was having a particularly tough time in life. It's a novel about hope, family and belonging. I've been supported over the years by so many people and I'm sorry if I have left anyone out.

To my agent Chloe Seager. Thanks for being so warm and helping me figure out what comes next.

Piccadilly Press – my novel is WAY better for your involvement. Thanks to the BEST editor Georgia Murray, for being a champion of the book from the start. To the rest of the team: Holly Kyte (copy-editor), Talya Baker (proofreader), Molly Holt (PR), Dominica Clements (cover designer), Dan Newman (text designer) – you've all been fab.

MASSIVE thanks to Anh Cao, who created a wonderful cover and internal art for the novel. I've enjoyed seeing Danny's drawing come into being through you.

Mrs Selwood (English teacher at school) – thank you for always encouraging me to find the words.

To Jonathan Davidson and team at Writing West Midlands – you have been supportive of me since the start. To Kit de Waal, who has been fantastic in her support of a fellow Brummie writer, and Sophie Morgan – you were there when I was writing the first draft of *Danny Chung*, and to Steph Vidal Hall – thanks for the creative coaching.

To my first creative writing tutors: Nicola Monaghan, Jackie Gay and Richard Beard. My fellow students who became great friends: Sophie, Rena, and Edmund.

Leila Rasheed from the Megaphone scheme, which changed my life. I had inklings that I could be a children's author and Megaphone has helped make that a reality. Thanks to Nafisa, Avanti, Danielle and Joyce, who made that year such a joy. As did Catherine Johnson, Patrice Lawrence, Candy Gourlay and Alex Wheatle, who came to speak to us; you paved the way for more writers of colour in the UK – you all rock.

Thanks to SCBWI friends: Sarah B., A. M. Dassu, Rashmi, B. B. Taylor, for checking in on me. And the Glasgow Children's Writers Group: Tita, Susan, Lindsay, Dean, Emily, Josh, Joey and Alistair.

And to Bubble Tea Writers: Yen, Eliza, Anne, Lui, Martin, Winnie, Mimi, Panni, Lu-Hai and loads more.

Thanks to Muhammed Khan (author and maths teacher) for his advice on the Fibonacci sequence.

To Alice S-H who saw something in my writing and Lisa Williamson for being very sweet and reading my very first novel.

To Creative Scotland and Peter Pan Moat Brae Trust for allowing me to be the Dr Gavin Wallace Fellow for a whole year. Also, thanks to Scottish Book Trust for being so welcoming when I moved to Scotland and Jenny Kumar from Literature Alliance.

It's always wonderful to have friends cheering you on. So, thank you to Ramona, Jane, Carmen, Eve, Eva, Antoine, Sarah, Cat, Csilla, Rhona P., Becks, Rhona M., Noy, Ruth and Ellen, as well as many others.

To my family, Jose, Santi and Alma – thanks for your love and support. I love ya!

MAISIE CHAN

Danny Chung Does Not Do Maths is Maisie's first novel. She lives in Glasgow with her Spanish husband and her two children. When Maisie isn't writing, she loves practising yoga, eating dim sum and trying to keep plants alive (she's not very green-fingered!). She grew up in a council house in Birmingham with other fostered children and lots of pets (dogs, cats, hamsters, rabbit, guinea pigs, budgies, tropical fish) and loves to write for children as it's the best job in the world. (She doesn't mind doing maths, but prefers writing instead.)

ANH CAO

Anh Cao is an illustrator originally from Ho Chi Minh City, Vietnam. After coming to the UK to study, she found her passion in drawing and decided to pursue her dream in art. She now works and lives in London, as an illustrator and visual development artist.

Thank you for choosing a Piccadilly Press book.

If you would like to know more about our
authors or our books, or if you'd just like to know
what we're up to, you can find us online.

www.piccadillypress.co.uk

And you can also find us on:

We hope to see you soon!